Silenced Night

Lori Altebaumer

Published by Lori Altebaumer, 2024.

To Mom and Dad

Chapter One

E ven though she'd been expecting the phone call, Everleigh Greene couldn't stop the heavy breath that seeped from her burdened soul.

"Your testimony is crucial to the case. I need you well rested and ready to go right after the holidays," the voice on the other end of the line said.

"I understand." She didn't have to like it, but she did understand it.

"And hey . . . Merry Christmas!" The call ended, leaving nothing but a buzzing in her ear.

Instead of relief, the call from the district attorney only stirred memories. Like an innocent breeze breathing new life into the embers of a dying fire, the coals of anxiety blazed hot once again, burning inside her chest.

The date was set. The trial would start the week after Christmas.

Christmas . . . the season of peace, joy, and goodwill toward men.

She shook her head. *Until your neighbor is brutally beaten on Christmas Eve and you're the only one who can link the suspect to the crime.*

She'd spent the past twelve months trying to shut out the images. Now she had one week until they would once again be ruthlessly dragged from her memories in all their bloody detail.

Closing the folder in front of her, she moved it to an empty corner of her desk. Last Christmas, she'd decorated her office with a tiny fake tree in that exact spot.

She tapped a stack of papers on the desk to straighten them then placed them on top of the folder.

Artificial trees and artificial holidays had no place in a world that spun on facts alone. Was her faith just as artificial?

The question hit her like the biting slap of a winter wind.

Her faith—or what there was of it—certainly hadn't brought her any peace.

With the date finally set, the DA and everyone else wanted to make sure the only eyewitness would be there. As if she had a choice.

Well, maybe not *everyone* wanted her there. Surely the accused would rather she disappear. Something a family with the resources his possessed could make happen if they really wanted to.

But she wanted to testify. Kariss Workman had spent the last year of her life comatose in a hospital bed. Surely Everleigh could endure a short time of unpleasant cross examination on the witness stand.

She kneaded her aching shoulders, knowing it wouldn't help.

When she'd identified the son of one of her employer's top clients—not to mention being the grandson of the town's beloved former pastor—as the person she saw climbing out of the neighbor's window, things had gotten awkward at work. So far, her job with the firm had survived, but it still had to endure the threshing floor of the witness stand Everleigh would soon face. She had no doubt the defense attorney planned to beat the wheat from the chaff with no regard to her future career plans.

She wanted justice for the poor girl who'd spent the past twelve months in a coma—and for the unborn baby who had died—but she could still hope her career along with her plans to grow roots in this town didn't become a third victim.

A knock on her office door made her jump.

"Merry Christmas!" Megan Lively entered, carrying a Christmassy paper dessert plate in one hand and a Styrofoam cup in the other.

"Who's the generous giver this time?"

"The better question is what, and the answer is the best fruitcake you've ever tasted. I'll sacrifice my quota of Christmas calories just to eat this and happily pay for it later." She set the cup and plate on the desk and pinched off another bite. "As long as I can still fit in my dress for the party."

Megan was as close to being everything a girl could hope to be as one could get. Tall, long blonde hair, attractive, intelligent, and perpetually in a good mood. In addition to being homecoming queen, prom queen, and class favorite, she'd also been voted Most Likely to Succeed. And for some reason, she'd taken Everleigh into her friendship.

Her only flaw, if it could be called one, was her taste for expensive things. Their jobs with the accounting firm paid well, but Everleigh still wasn't sure how Megan afforded the Mustang convertible, designer clothes, and endless array of Kendra Scott jewelry she indulged in. Credit card debt, she suspected.

Megan slid the plate toward her.

Everleigh picked it up and moved it to the credenza behind her. "I'll save it for later. But," she lifted the cup and inhaled, "I'll gladly accept this hot apple cider."

From Thanksgiving to Christmas, the break room contained a variety of Christmas-spirited food items from clients of the accounting firm—the perfect gift for people already struggling against the effects of a sedentary job. Everleigh made a note to park at the far end of the lot for the rest of the season.

"I've been asked to remind you that your RSVP for the Taylors' annual Christmas party at the Country Club hasn't been received. You aren't thinking of skipping it, are you?" A perfectly sculpted eyebrow rose to a point above fake eyelashes.

Megan put her hands on slender, shapely hips, manicured fingernails resembling glittery daggers spread out across her flat abdomen. "You're not going to miss this. The Taylors are one of our biggest clients, and they adore you. Plus, if you want to fit in around here, you've got to make more effort. It's been almost two years since you took this job, and a year since the . . . Well, all you ever do is work. The Taylors' Christmas party is the place to start."

Everleigh propped her elbow on her desk and cradled her chin in her palm. Arguing with her coworker was pointless, but maybe Megan would go away if she stalled long enough.

"I know it's been a rough year. But you can't help what you saw." Megan's gaze drifted down then floated back up as though carried on an uncertain breeze. "You're still sure that's what you saw, right?"

Megan had never questioned her before. No one in their right mind would go through this just for the attention. "Quite."

"Good. But the way you've been hiding out isn't helping. So," Megan swept her hair over her shoulder, which Everleigh had come to believe was the main reason she wore it long and straight, "I'll tell them that you're coming. Should I put you down for a plus-one? I can help with that."

"No plus-one." The only thing worse than being at a party she didn't want to go to was being there with a stranger she didn't want to be with.

"And tell me you have something to wear that isn't quite so vanilla. The grayscale look is fine for the office, but this is a party. You need something with color." Megan cocked her head to the side, giving Everleigh an assessing look, no doubt considering how she might transform Everleigh's blockish shape into something more appealing through the magic of fabric.

An impossible task. Everleigh had been down this path before.

"I have the perfect thing."

"You do realize we aren't the same size, right?" Everleigh glanced at her own unpolished, closely trimmed nails before tucking her hands beneath her desk. Size wasn't the only thing they didn't have in common.

"But you and my little sister are. The dress she wore as homecoming queen is perfect." She beamed as if she'd just been promoted to head fairy godmother, then slid into the next topic of conversation as though the matter were settled. "Are you ready for our trip tomorrow?"

Everleigh's mouth moved into something that felt like a combination grimace and grin. A weekend at the lake house belonging to Megan's parents would be nice. Time away from the Christmas joy oozing over everything she saw and out of everyone she met. The phone call from the DA had incinerated any holiday enthusiasm she might have had, reducing it to a wispy pile of ash.

Her heart wasn't into anything but getting the trial behind her. "I'll pack tonight."

"And change of plans. I'll pick you up at your place at eight. Don't be late. I, for one, am ready for a change of scenery." Once again, she flipped her hair over her shoulder, using both hands this time. She batted her dark lashes. "Now I need a favor. Would you swap days for cleaning the breakroom?" Megan's tone was half begging, half already out the door because she knew Everleigh would say yes.

"Sure." Staying busy helped time pass faster, and Everleigh had nothing but an empty house and unpleasant thoughts to go home to anyway.

At five thirty, the usual time she allowed herself to leave work, she headed to the break room to clean up.

She covered the partially eaten fruitcake in plastic wrap before washing the butcher knife they had cut the cake with and a pile of miscellaneous cups waiting for her in the sink. Finally, she wiped down the counters. The activity soothed her. The kitchen had always been her refuge. She missed the Christmas baking she used to enjoy. This kitchen didn't have a stove or oven like at her house.

It also didn't have a window out of which to see things she couldn't forget.

She didn't doubt what she'd seen, so why did thoughts of the upcoming trial make her knees feel ready to buckle?

A half hour later, Everleigh dropped the slice of unwanted fruitcake into the trash and headed to the parking lot.

It would all be over soon, right?

Justice would be served.

Not that it would make things right again. An unborn infant had died, a young woman still lay in a coma, and a man might go to prison. God might have sent a Savior into the world two thousand years ago, but He hadn't done much saving as far as Everleigh could see.

Chapter Two

Everleigh checked the rearview mirror and tightened her grip on the steering wheel to stop the tremor in her hands. She should have eaten the fruitcake. This must be low blood sugar, not growing paranoia that someone was following her. Better to have eaten the fruitcake than to feel like one.

She changed lanes, moving to the right. The black SUV had dropped three cars back, but it wasn't long before it appeared in the right lane.

Before she panicked, she'd try one more thing. Waiting until the last second, she flipped on her blinker. Her tires squealed as she swung into the parking lot of her favorite fast food, taking her place at the end of the long drive-through line.

A measure of tension slipped from the death-like grip she held on the steering wheel when the SUV drove on. Fast food might not be the remedy for paranoia, but it would make the experience more enjoyable. She'd even pick up an order for Charlie, her elderly neighbor, along with his favorite large lemonade. He didn't need to know he was getting the diet version thanks to his recent diabetes diagnosis.

Traffic had thinned from the frenetic rush of evening commuters when she pulled out of the parking lot. The aroma of the bacon cheeseburgers and hot fries filled her car. She plucked a fry from the paper bag and savored the crisp, salty perfection as she waited for the light to turn green.

The SUV was nowhere around. The fries she snitched from the bag worked miracles in restoring her perspective. No more skipping lunch—at least not until the trial ended.

She considered calling Charlie before he had time to open another can of SpaghettiOs—his usual dinner and another dietary habit he needed to change.

Fifteen minutes later, she turned down the street lined with Christmas lights and festive decorations. Trees decked out like the debutantes of December stared from living room windows as if to say, "Merry Christmas . . . but not for you Everleigh Greene."

The neighborhood had felt decidedly unneighborly since last Christmas.

Only one dark spot existed on the street, two unlit houses side by side. One had the excuse of being vacant with no happy occupant to decorate it. The other was Everleigh's.

Even Charlie had strung up multi-colored lights in an uneven fashion around his porch and attached a wreath to the front door.

The Craftsman-style fixer-upper she called home had been love at first sight when Everleigh found it. A home to make her own. Her first daydreams for the place had centered around Christmases to come.

Now instead of decorating for the holidays, she found herself contemplating something much less merry—selling. That's what the Greenes did, right? Move on when life didn't suit them.

The notion hadn't yet progressed into action. After all, there was Charlie.

And her fierce determination to find stability. She wouldn't run . . . not yet.

She parked the car in her driveway and studied the joyless little home set among the riot of lights illuminating the rest of the street. It almost looked sad, as if it had a soul in mourning, jealous of the other homes and their festivities, but too traumatized to trust the season.

With the bag of fast food in one hand and Charlie's lemonade in the other, she closed the car door with a hip bump and headed across the street to the house of her elderly friend.

The street that separated their homes curved up a hill—more of a large bump of earth—behind his house. His ranch-style home sat with its back to the hill, forcing it to also sit at an angle as though it were turning a cold shoulder to the street. A little higher than the rest of the houses, between the angle and the elevation, his home gave Everleigh the impression it guarded the neighborhood and all who lived here. Last Christmas she'd discovered that was a faulty impression.

A widower, Charlie Douglas no longer got around much thanks to his arthritis. In good weather, Charlie spent long hours on his porch. When he wasn't there, he waved at her from his window. Affection rose within her like the yeasty dough for Christmas morning cinnamon rolls. The angst tugging the corners of her lips down lessened. Charlie's friendship was like those rolls—sweet, comforting. Their aroma alone promised something wonderful to come.

She knocked then turned the knob—unlocked. She'd lectured him before about keeping his door locked, but it hadn't made him change his ways.

"It's Everleigh," she called as she headed to the kitchen where she found him holding an unopened can of SpaghettiOs in one hand. He stared at the can opener in his other with a look that bordered on bewilderment. "I brought you some supper."

"You're just in time." He spotted the sack then grinned like a little boy who'd been handed an all season pass to the carnival. "I'll just put these in the . . ." He paused, appearing uncertain.

Frowning, Everleigh took the can from his hand. "Let me." She returned the can and the opener to their proper places.

"Did I tell you my grandson will be here tomorrow?" Charlie abandoned his place by the stove. He shuffled around a kitchen still arranged exactly like the late Mrs. Douglas had left it.

She turned off the forgotten stove burner while he fussed around extricating supper from the bag.

He reached to pull two plates from the cabinet, and she stopped him.

"I can't stay." It was mostly a lie, which she wasn't proud of. She wasn't in the mood for company tonight—not even Charlie's.

A look of disappointment flickered over his face. Guilt zinged through her.

"How long will your grandson stay?" She redirected the conversation, ignoring the squeezing sensation in her chest. She should be happy for him to have family around for the holidays. Just because she'd be alone—again—was no reason to wish that on anyone else.

Besides, no obligations for Christmas gave her another day to work. She'd need to get ahead before the trial started, just in case.

"He'll be here through the New Year while he recovers from his . . . shoulder surgery. Of course, he probably just thinks this ol' coot needs someone to watch after him." He winked. "Reckon I ought to tell him my new neighbor does a right fine job of that."

"I think you've got it backwards. It's you who keeps an eye on me."

"Be easier for both of us then if you'd stay for supper."

Everleigh exhaled in mock exasperation. "Fine. But this time I insist on doing the dishes, and I'm not staying to watch reruns of *The Rockford Files*."

He chuckled as he set a second plate on the table. "*Kojak*?"

"Fine, *The Rockford Files*. And you know we could save the dishes and just eat out of the containers." It was the same argument they always had.

"My Anna wouldn't have it, serving a lady by making 'em eat out of the to-go containers." He paused and looked down at the table. "My Anna, she should've had every meal on fine china with polished silver and fancy crystal glasses." His voice broke as his gaze drifted back into something Everleigh couldn't see. It offered a rare glimpse into his loneliness.

An hour and a half later, Everleigh put away the last of the dishes she'd cleaned, tucked a throw blanket around Charlie, then clicked off the TV, silencing the rerun of his favorite show. She stood for a moment, pondering what life must have been like in this house. While she'd had a loving home, with two career military parents, it had never been stable. For the most part, she'd been raised by a somewhat eccentric grandmother with a bad case of wanderlust.

And a reputation as the village crazy. Chagrin snaked around her at the memory.

A part of her longed to know what it would feel like to be someone's "Anna." Although she didn't imagine herself the kind of woman who could earn such adoration from a good man like Charlie Douglas.

A bite in the night air nipped at her cheeks when she stepped onto the porch. She locked and closed the door, cutting off the sound of her neighbor's gentle snoring. She shivered, hugging herself against the cold.

Apprehension skittered over her. She could go back and wake Charlie, ask him to watch out while she inspected her house. But she didn't want to disrupt his sleep or ruin a pleasant evening by revealing that she didn't feel safe and hadn't since that night over a year ago.

Stupid, she told herself. The police believed it was an intentional act of violence aimed at a specific person. But images of that night still chilled her in a way no winter wind ever could.

She rubbed her arms as she stepped from the soft glow from the lights draped around Charlie's porch. The slight curve of the hill created a thin strip of dark that sliced its way between his house and hers.

Silence hung over the neighborhood tonight, and her steps made crisp, clicking sounds as she crossed the street. An engine revved from somewhere near the top of the hill. Everleigh looked up. Headlights grew larger as though flying toward her, blinding her. Panic shot through her veins. She lunged for her yard.

Her toe caught on the curb, and she tumbled head-first into the grass.

She sat up, a burning pain twisting through her ankle. That wasn't her biggest concern though. Had someone just tried to run her over?

Her own car blocked her view as the other car sped away, the angry sound of its engine fading.

She might have been able to convince herself the driver hadn't seen her. Might . . . if it weren't a black SUV she'd glimpsed as she fell.

Chapter Three

Everleigh tapped her fingers against the steering wheel in time to the tune of "Jingle Bells."

The unease she'd experienced last Friday had evaporated faster than a Texas snowflake as she'd hiked—or more accurately hobbled—through the juniper and oak covered hills surrounding Megan's family's lake property. The fresh air and time away had soothed her soul, if not her tender ankle.

A Monday immersed in numbers and accounting reports had followed. Orderly, controlled, and just the distraction she needed.

It had her almost humming along to the Christmas carols on the radio as she navigated the evening drive home.

When she looked in the rearview mirror today, the only thing concerning was the red dress draped over the back seat. The one Megan borrowed from her sister. The one missing half the bottom and a decent portion of the top. She hadn't been able to say no after receiving a free weekend getaway.

No way she would set foot outside her house in that dress.

One quick swish of the short lacy skirt would erase every bit of respect she'd worked hard to earn. Overcoming her flighty upbringing demanded diligence in every area of her life, especially her work life if she wanted the stability that success could offer her.

With no desire for a shopping expedition, she'd have to scrounge up something passable from her closet. Humming along to Christmas carols wasn't the same as encountering the full force of holiday cheer she would find in the hyper-commercialized world of retail.

The song on the radio changed. She jabbed the radio control, ending the gentle, rolling refrain of "Silent Night." The lyrics had become a mockery she couldn't hum along to anymore.

What good was the birth of a Savior who wasn't saving innocent people from the depravity of the wicked?

Her good mood now slid down the grief-lined path toward despair.

A truck parked in front of Charlie's house drop-kicked her disposition deeper into the gloom. Charlie's grandson. A "Silent Night" indeed now that she didn't have Charlie for a refuge. An unreasonable pinch nipped her heart. Without intending to, she'd laid claim to Charlie, and she didn't like sharing.

She parked, then fumbled in the cupholder for her keys only to find them in her coat pocket. She was halfway to her front door when she realized something was wrong.

A large evergreen rested on her porch where a large evergreen shouldn't be. Even more concerning was the man seated on the swing where he shouldn't be either.

She glanced at Charlie's house then remembered he wouldn't be watching from his window. He'd have better things to do with his grandson in town. She could dive back into her car and probably get the door closed before he reached her. Instead, she checked her watch. Not yet six p.m. Too early in the evening for stalkers. Probably.

"I'm afraid you're at the wrong house. Who're you looking for?" The idea of a Christmas tree delivery charmed her, though it didn't change her mind about getting one. Especially not if it came with delivery men who loitered around on porches scaring the daylights out of people.

"Nope. I'm right where I planned to be, Miss Everleigh Greene." His five o'clock shadow shifted into a pleasingly masculine grin she didn't need much light to detect.

She opened her mouth to correct him, then snapped it shut when she realized he'd said her name. Alarm tingled up her arms. "Do I know you?"

"Not yet."

She scowled. Dressed in loose-fitting Levi's and an untucked flannel shirt that hung open over a faded Henley, he looked like he'd just stepped off the set of a Hallmark movie. The scuffed work boots he wore rested on her porch, rocking the swing in a relaxed rhythm that didn't match the accelerated beating of her heart.

Nothing about him made her feel threatened, especially with one of his arms in a sling. Annoyed maybe, but that was a different matter.

Despite what had happened here, people in this town generally still trusted one another. Even so, when he didn't say more, she slid one hand into the coat pocket where her cell phone resided. Her other hand worked the keys she held through her fingers, forming the closest thing to a weapon she could think of.

"Seriously, can I help you?" If she wanted a Christmas tree and a good-looking man on her porch, she would get them herself. And he still hadn't introduced himself.

"Actually, I'm here to help you. I found myself with an extra tree and thought maybe you'd like it since I noticed you haven't decorated," he made a show of looking down the street at the other houses, "like everyone else in the neighborhood. Sure way to get yourself left off the invite list for the block party next Fourth of July."

If her neighbors wanted to judge her for not decorating for Christmas, so be it. People really should get their priorities in order.

"You're aware that yours is the only occupied house on this street without a single bit of decoration, right?"

"I'm aware." She shifted her stance as though it might block his view of the competition. "But I don't need your tree, so you can give it to someone else."

"No one *needs* a tree. It's just fun." Planting his feet, he stilled the swing, "And I didn't mean to offend you."

"I'm not offended. I'm bothered." And that *bothered* her even more because Everleigh Greene did not get *bothered* easily. At least, not that she showed.

"And annoyed?"

"Now that you mention it, yes."

"Uh huh." The good-natured look he wore faded into something she couldn't interpret. He stared as though he were looking at some mythical creature . . . a woman who didn't like Christmas.

Everleigh didn't like being judged. She liked being misjudged even less.

"So, Mr. He-Who-Shall-Not-Be-Named, how do I convince you to take your tree and leave?" Her words came with precision, her shoulders stiffening as her chin tipped up. She knew she'd never met him before. His face was not one to be forgotten. She cleared her throat, noting it suddenly felt like the August Texas sun blazed down on her. Her reaction to him unsettled her.

The fact he still hadn't introduced himself negated any sense of hospitality she might have felt.

Amusement danced across his features.

"Take the tree and *leaf*?" He raised his eyebrows as though encouraging her to laugh with him.

"Okay . . . that wasn't exactly what I meant." She tried not to smile. "But it's really not that funny either."

In the days since the attack next door, she'd become guarded. She wanted a reason to let that guard down, but she couldn't risk it, not now. And not with a handsome and mysterious tree bearing stranger. "Look, I appreciate the offer, but I really don't have time."

"I agree. Christmas is less than a week away. No time to waste."

"I'm not in the mood for Christmas this year."

"Putting up a Christmas tree would change that. Besides, I bought it from the police department fundraiser, so the money went to a worthy cause." He stood, sliding his free hand into his pocket. "Would it change your mind to know that I also brought a whole box of lights and ornaments? We could have this thing up and decorated in no time."

"Appreciate the thoughtfulness, just not this year." She had relinquished her hand full of keys and now crossed her arms, more agitated than afraid. The nerve of a stranger to not only pick out a tree on her behalf but invite himself to decorate it. "And really, Father Christmas, why are you so concerned about whether I decorate?"

He shrugged. "Honestly can't say that I am, but I was told to bring you Christmas cheer."

"Told by whom? And don't say Santa Claus."

"Almost, but not quite. Mind if I ask you a personal question?" He studied her with more than a casual interest and Everleigh stiffened. "How's your faith?"

"Excuse me." Offense ruffled along her spine. Her answer to his question wasn't so good right now. She felt further from God than she had since she'd given her life to Him. But she wasn't about to have that discussion with a stranger, no matter how much the look he wore threatened to melt her all the way down to the marrow of her bones. Deep set, dark eyes in a finely chiseled face framed by just the right amount of five o'clock shadow. *Everleigh, you are not that shallow. Focus.* "That's none of your business."

"It should be everybody's business, don't you think?"

No arguing that point, but she wasn't interested in receiving a sermon while standing in the middle of her yard. She studied the tree until the conviction over the shabby state of her faith faded, then pinned him with the stare that usually sent men on their way. "Are you going to leave now? Or do I need to call the police?"

She'd rather decorate every square inch of her house than call the police. The last time she'd made such a call her life had turned into a nightmare she still hadn't fully recovered from.

"Well, I guess you could do that." He reached up to scratch his chin, a slight grin toying with the corners of his mouth. "I suppose if I can't talk you into accepting this tree, I'll just have to toss it in the woodchipper and put it in the compost pile. Seems like a waste of such a beautiful thing."

Everleigh rocked up on her toes and back down again. Caught in the path of a look she couldn't fathom, she fought the urge to squirm. The heat inched up by several degrees, covering her from head to toe with the sensation he was talking about more than the tree.

She smothered the wayward—and likely erroneous—thought.

It was a pretty tree. And she did love the smell of pine, like the evergreens she was named after. "Well . . . "

"Great. I can bring it in for you, although I'm thinking you'll say you don't let men you don't know inside your house. And to that I will reply that we're neighbors."

"Neighbors usually introduce themselves."

"Point made. I'm Luke Douglas."

"So you're . . . "

"Charlie's grandson."

Everleigh looked across the street to Charlie's house. "This was Charlie's idea? You could have told me that to start with."

"I wanted to see what kind of female Grandpa is keeping company with."

Everleigh's head snapped back to find him teasing her. The expression he wore now danced over her heart.

"Okay, Mr. Douglas. I'll keep the tree under two conditions. One, I won't promise to decorate it. And two, you *will* promise to haul it away right after Christmas."

He grinned, a sparkle in his eyes. With the memory of those eyes, she wouldn't need lights on her tree.

She met him on the porch, and he extended his hand for the shake that would make it official.

An unexpected pleasure radiated up her arm at the feel of her hand in his.

Did he hold her hand a bit longer than necessary? She flushed, turning her attention to the tree behind him instead of the keen look he gave her.

Then he sobered, his demeanor shifting so visibly it drew hers right along with it. "Now that I've done what Charlie asked me to do, I need to ask you something more serious." He leaned the tree aside. "Do you often get your mail like this?"

The sight made her breath hitch. A knife impaled a Christmas card to the antique wooden door she'd worked all summer to restore. Her hand shot up to cover her neck.

"Judging by your response, I'm going to say it's not the first such note you've received."

"The last one was only wedged into the doorframe." And it was almost a year ago . . . right after that terrible night. Just a childish prank from some neighborhood kids.

"Want to explain?"

"It's nothing."

"It's a threat against your life."

"Isn't it a crime to read other people's mail?"

"I think there's some gray area when it's stuck to their door with a butcher knife."

Everleigh moved closer to read the words. The same message as before.

"Do you have any idea who did this?" Luke asked.

"Just neighborhood kids playing pranks."

"You sure about that?"

Everleigh hesitated. She'd brought on enough trouble by identifying culprits.

"Any idea why someone might want to scare you?"

"Maybe." That she did know. But she'd keep it to herself. She refused to accept any other explanation than childish mischief.

He pulled a latex glove from his back pocket and worked his hand into it. No small accomplishment given the sling he wore limited the use of his left hand.

"Did you just pull a glove from your pocket?"

"Yes." He dislodged the knife from the door.

"Why?"

"I'd like to have it checked for fingerprints, and if any are found I'd like for them not to be mine."

"You can just take things to the police and have them check for fingerprints? And why do you carry latex gloves in your pockets?" She tried to recall if Charlie had ever mentioned what his grandson did for a living.

"I know some people who owe me favors." He nodded toward his truck across the street. "And I don't keep gloves in my pocket. I keep them in my truck." He pulled a couple of plastic bags from another pocket.

He placed the knife in one bag and the card in another, but not before Everleigh got one last look at the words written in blood red.

Wishing you a silenced night.

Chapter Four

T he sun hadn't yet edged its way up over the horizon as Luke sipped his coffee from Charlie's front porch. But he wasn't watching the horizon. He was watching the house across the street.

She'd let him take the knife and the note under the condition he tell her anything he found out first. As in no going to parents of potential juvenile offenders without her approval. Fortunately for him, she'd only made it a condition. He hadn't been required to promise anything. A giant loophole he'd feel only a moment's worth of guilt about exploiting if he felt the need.

What Luke hadn't mentioned—and there was a decently long list of things he'd omitted—was his concern this might be witness intimidation. From what he knew, her testimony was crucial to the prosecution. If she recognized the threatening tone of this message, she might do exactly what they intended—change her story or recant altogether.

He also didn't want to take a chance she might unwillingly disappear altogether.

If she wanted to believe in her neighborhood pranksters theory, that might be for the best. At least until something more threatening turned up.

He shook his head. How much more threatening could it be than a Christmas card stuck to the door with a butcher knife? His gut grappled with a hunch this wouldn't be the end. Charlie's neighbor could be in serious danger.

She wasn't comfortable with the questions he'd left unanswered. He'd seen it in her eyes. Green eyes that sparkled like gypsum and melted his heart faster than a Texas snowman at noon when she aimed them at him.

His lips quirked as though he might smile, but guilt for his deception squashed the pleasure. She didn't appear to know what he did for a living. What chance did he have once she did? She'd all but admitted to a lack of faith last night.

He should've been honest with her. He was a detective who'd just spent the past eighteen months working deep undercover. Until he'd been shot. Now he was here with Charlie under the pretext of recovering from a shoulder surgery. Not a lie. He did have shoulder surgery, but it was to pull a piece of lead out and not to repair a torn rotator cuff like everyone assumed.

Unfortunately, his wounded shoulder wasn't the only thing he needed to recover from. The bullet he'd taken in the flesh had destroyed more than just soft tissue. It had been the final straw that drove the woman he'd been dating to end the relationship. The stress was too much for her.

Would it be that way with every woman he met? Would he have to give up his career to have the kind of love his grandparents had?

Unequally yoked Charlie had said. Luke knew his grandpa was right, but he'd had to chew on it for a few days before he could make peace with it. She'd been more in love with her dreams than she'd been with God. The neat future she'd planned out didn't include worrying whether her husband would come home after each shift. The bullet meant to kill him had instead taken out their relationship. With only herself and her false sense of control to cling to, she'd fallen prey to fear.

The woman who could love a man who did the things he did would need to have a strong faith in something besides herself—or him.

He scratched the top of his head as if he could reach through his skull and thump his brain. He'd asked the first woman he'd noticed since the breakup how her faith was. *What kind of idiot had he become?*

He knew what happened here last Christmas. And he knew that Charlie worried about his attractive neighbor. A worry that had nothing to do with threatening notes and butcher knives.

Charlie hadn't exactly said *attractive*. Luke had deduced that bit of information for himself. He was a pretty darn good detective, after all.

When his grandpa expressed concern because she hadn't put up a single Christmas decoration, Luke had decided to do his grandpa a favor for both their benefit. He'd reach out with an olive branch . . . or in this case, a Christmas tree.

But he wanted her to know she could count on him to protect her.

So why hadn't he just come out and said it?

Because when he'd lost himself in her eyes, he'd found a guarded vulnerability that had swept his common sense away.

That and enough experience to make him cautious.

He was attracted to her, and he wanted a chance for her to like him before she fell in love with the badge . . . or ran in the opposite direction.

And before he let her like him, he'd need to know the strength of her faith.

Chapter Five

Everleigh pressed her face into her palms, exhaled, then lifted her head to examine the spreadsheet again. She sipped the cup of coffee that had cooled to room temperature hours ago. Something didn't add up. No way she'd made such sloppy mistakes.

"Knock, knock." Megan bubbled into Everleigh's office like soda fizz, as giddy as though she were handing out candy canes made of silver and gold. Instead, she waved a swag of emerald in front of Everleigh. Another dress with considerably more fabric. "Surprise."

Everleigh arched an eyebrow, questioning. She'd found the courage to be honest about the first dress. She hadn't expected a second offering.

The rich green velvet glistened beneath the fluorescent lights. With a full skirt, stitched in layers like a Roman coliseum, a square neckline, and sleeves that puffed more than Everleigh liked, it certainly qualified as a more modest dress.

"What do you think?"

"I think it's . . . "

"Matronly? Borderline frumpy? Flat-out hideous?"

"I was going to say unusual for today's style. Maybe kind of retro."

Megan laughed. "It should be. It's my mother's." She draped the dress over the back of an empty chair. "There you have it, Everleigh. You can go to the party in something modern and sexy that'll make heads turn. Or you can wear this."

"Or I could just not go."

"Too late. Already RSVP'd." Megan swished her hair back over her shoulder. "But there's still time for a plus-one. My cousin will be here. He'd make a perfect date." She frowned. "Although I would have to insist you wear the red dress, so it doesn't look like he's on a date with his aunt."

"Or I could just not go."

Megan turned and headed out the door, calling over her shoulder, "You're going."

Everleigh stared into the cold, black liquid in the cup she held. Which dress would Luke like best?

The haste with which she set the cup down caused the unappealing liquid to slosh onto the papers fanned across the desktop. She swiped it away, frustrated by the dark smudges on her previously pristine spreadsheet.

She knew the answer, but she didn't like it. What man wouldn't prefer the more revealing—dare she say *sexier*—outfit? Sexy wasn't her goal. She would make her way in the world with her brain and not her body. She tugged at the hem of her shirt, stretching out the folds of fabric that had bunched around her middle. *As if you have a choice.*

The real source of her aggravation was that the thought had even crossed her mind. Focused, determined, success-oriented women didn't contemplate such matters as men's tastes in dress choices. And they certainly didn't swoon over men they'd just met.

Did she just use the word *swoon*? Maybe the green dress was the right choice for her after all.

Besides, she could wear a sensible pair of flats with the matronly looking dress now residing in the empty chair across from her. The fewer heads that turned in her direction, the better.

The party was tomorrow night.

The trial started next week.

They both held the same appeal. She'd be forced to be the center of attention at one. She didn't plan to be so at the other.

THE SECURITY GUARD at the front gate checked her name on the guest list and waved Everleigh into an almost full parking lot.

She tucked her phone and keys in her coat pocket then headed into what she anticipated being ninety minutes of discomfort masquerading as a Christmas party. She'd promised Megan ninety minutes and nothing more. It had been the only way to get her to drop the subject over lunch today.

The evening air nipped at her cheeks, and she hugged her coat closed against her chest.

Tiny white lights strung along the edge of the sidewalk created an atmosphere of enchantment.

The feeling of peace settled over her. That's what Christmas was all about, right? Maybe it was time to trust it again.

She stopped, squaring her shoulders as she released the grip she had on her coat. It wasn't the shield of a gladiator, and she wasn't heading into the arena to fight the lions. It was a Christmas party, for Pete's sake, and she was a capable, confident adult. With chin lifted, she resumed her course, repeating the words *you belong* in the hope she might actually believe it.

The valet in a crisp black tuxedo greeted her with the smile his employer paid him to give everyone as he opened the door with a slight bow. "Enjoy your evening."

"I doubt it." Everleigh whispered the words to herself.

Sparkle and glitter and shine in a theme of gold and white engulfed her, overwhelming her senses. It was like stepping into a fairy tale. As if Prince Charming might be waiting just around the corner. The image of Luke's face jostled her thoughts, and she almost let herself wonder what it would be like to be here with him tonight. Almost.

"You made it!" Megan rushed to embrace her as though she feared Everleigh might turn and run. Her friend leaned back and frowned. "And I see you chose the . . . uhmmm . . . well, this dress."

Disapproval laced her words as she helped Everleigh out of her coat, turning to hand it to the coat check before Everleigh could stop her. The lady behind the counter wore a no-nonsense look that beckoned Everleigh's trust. Her coat and the contents of her pockets should be fine. Although if she'd known she'd have to relinquish it, she'd have carried her purse—matching or not.

Megan took her hand and pulled her toward the reception hall. A gust of chilly night air swept in with the sound of the door opening, attracting Everleigh's attention.

What she saw made her lungs reach up her throat to snatch her last breath back. Her feet became anchors holding her in place. He must have been close behind her as she walked alone through the parking lot. Chills rocketed up her spine.

Megan tugged her arm, her polished nails digging into Everleigh's flesh. "Come on. Let's check out the mistletoe martinis. I hear they're to die for."

Everleigh scowled, but the distraction freed her steps.

"Sorry. Poor choice of words." Megan bit her lip.

"Why is he here? Why would anyone invite him *to a Christmas party*?" She let her friend pull her into the crowded reception hall while she mentally processed what she had seen. She planted her feet. "I have to go. I can't stay here."

"No." Megan's words hissed through the gaiety around them. "You deserve to be here. You can't let him intimidate you. Besides, you'll be safer here than out there alone."

"Surely there's some sort of rule that we can't be at the same event."

"You've spent the past year living like a recluse because you're afraid of a confrontation. I'm putting my foot down. Look at this place. It's gorgeous. The food is amazing. And for a woman in an old lady dress, you look stunning. Tonight, we celebrate the end of an awful year and the beginning of something new." Megan had her hands on her hips, her lips pressed into a thin line that said the subject was closed. But she also wasn't making eye contact. "Now let's get one of those martinis."

Once again, Megan gripped Everleigh's arm, dragging her along.

"Just water." Even if she had been one to enjoy mixed drinks, she wouldn't dare tonight. Not with Justin Wicketts anywhere around.

A half hour later, Everleigh stood with her fourth empty glass of water, regretting her lack of self-control. Abandoned by Megan, who was now engaged in a flirtatious conversation with the handsome local attorney, Everleigh's nervous energy transferred to sipping water at a rate a camel would have admired.

She searched the crowd once more, but Justin was nowhere to be found. In fact, she hadn't seen him again since that first moment in the foyer.

Maybe he'd been turned away. Did that make her feel any better? Now he knew where she was, but she didn't have the same knowledge about him.

She'd promised Megan an hour and a half. She hadn't promised where she'd spend the time. Now looked like a good time to visit the ladies' room.

After wasting as much time as she could there, she paused in the hallway to admire the Western paintings lining the hallways.

"Oh!" A woman's distressed voice carried from around the corner at the far end of the hall.

Soft crying followed, drawing her toward the sound.

"I'm lost. Don't leave me."

The thin, frightened voice tugged at Everleigh's heart, a reminder of her grandmother's decline into dementia.

She rounded a corner into the dark of an unlit passage. A thin slice of light radiated from an open door halfway down the hall. The crying had stopped, but she couldn't leave until she knew for sure the person was okay. She would have wanted someone to do that for her grandmother, and she would do it for Charlie.

The open door led into a janitor's closet filled with mop buckets and shelves stacked with cleaning supplies. She eased in for a better look. The prickly feel of apprehension lifted her hair a second before the door shut behind her.

She spun and grabbed the doorknob. Locked. "Hey! I'm in here." She pushed against the door, then pounded on it with her fist. Her hand stilled mid-swing on the third strike.

Maybe this wasn't an accident.

Stepping away from the door, she surveyed her surroundings.

She needed to formulate a plan in case they returned.

Formulate a plan?

She was an accountant, a number cruncher, a bean counter for Pete's sake. A pencil pusher with spaghetti arms in a stupid green dress at a party she never wanted to attend.

The only plan she'd ever formulated was how to minimize a capital gains tax.

She pressed her back against the wall.

Someone who would benefit from her silence had seen her here tonight.

How long before he returned?

Chapter Six

L uke spotted Everleigh's car parked at the far end of the empty lot. The front gate had been unmanned, a fact that didn't sit well. The cold knot growing in his midsection ever since his grandpa had shared his concerns gained about ten pounds.

Charlie couldn't be convinced Everleigh might have left early for work this morning. But when she hadn't answered Charlie's call, Luke's apprehension ticked up.

His grandpa had told him about the party she attended last night. Luke considered the possibility she'd hooked up with someone—maybe a date—and hadn't made it home yet. That possibility annoyed him more than it should have considering he'd only met her once. But he had to admit, based on everything his grandpa told him, he had higher expectations for her. One of these days he might have to lower the bar, or he'd end up alone for the rest of his life. But he wasn't there yet.

Charlie wouldn't rest until Luke either produced Everleigh physically or came up with a satisfactory explanation for her whereabouts. Luke grinned. The old man's attachment to his neighbor was kind of cute. So cute that he wasn't about to share his suspicion she might be having a one-night stand. Charlie insisted she didn't have a boyfriend and didn't date, so that was all it could be, right?

As if he'd read Luke's mind, Charlie had also implied in a not-so-subtle manner that Everleigh wasn't that kind of girl.

Truth was, after what Luke found on her door when he delivered the tree, Charlie's concern was justified.

He pulled his truck next to her car and double checked the Sig 9mm he carried in his side holster. He let his untucked flannel shirt drift over the firearm before stepping out to inspect her vehicle. The doors were locked, and she wasn't inside. It was an occupational hazard that his gaze went to the trunk. He shook his head. He wouldn't go down that line of thought yet.

The light from inside the expansive single-story building filtered into the pale morning. The early shift gearing up for the day. He gave the front door a tug. Locked. He skirted around the side, searching for a service entrance. Not that he expected to find her here. He doubted she could've spent the night inside the club unnoticed.

Which meant the most logical conclusion was that she'd gone home with someone. The thought soured in his empty stomach.

Wishing you a silenced night. The words on the card came back to him.

It hadn't yet been twenty-four hours but considering the note he'd seen and the fact she was a key witness in a murder and aggravated assault trial starting in a matter of days, there was more than enough reason to be cautious.

He moved from one door to the next, finding each one locked. As he reached for the third one, voices from the other side of the door roused his attention.

"Where do you think you're going? You're supposed to be vacuuming the dining room. You aren't any tireder than the rest of us who worked last night." A woman's stern voice carried through the closed metal door. A second voice mumbled something Luke couldn't make out.

He knocked on the door, waited half a second, then pounded again.

"Hold your horses. I'm coming." The door edged open to reveal a thin woman with a long gray ponytail and a no-nonsense expression.

The smell of hot coffee and freshly baked cinnamon rolls wafted out of the kitchen behind her as she studied him with the thoroughness of a prison warden. "We don't take deliveries here, and the office won't be open for another hour."

He braced his palm against the door, stopping her from closing it in his face.

"I'm looking for a friend. She attended an event here last night and didn't come home. Her car's out front. I'd like to look around if you don't mind."

Her eyes did that flicker thing that went from sudden understanding back to guardedness. His line of work made him all too familiar with that response. "Before I have to call the cops and report her missing, get everybody out looking for her where she was last seen."

That usually did the trick. Nobody wanted that attention or aggravation, so unless they were hiding something, they usually said yes.

He sensed her hesitation. Most likely she didn't have enough authority to make these kinds of decisions. She was weighing out what her boss would do if she refused and the cops showed up.

On further observation though, Luke realized it was worry clouding her face.

"Wait right here."

Luke scowled. Waiting wasn't his forte, but he stayed where she left him, contemplating his next move if she didn't return. Or returned and refused to let him in.

He didn't have to wait long.

She reappeared carrying a coat. "Is this hers?"

It looked like the one Everleigh had worn the night he met her, but he couldn't say for sure. Her coat wasn't the thing he'd been most interested in during their brief time together.

"She left it here last night in the coat check. Which happens sometimes when they've had too much to drink, and well . . . you know."

"No, I don't know. Why don't you tell me."

"When they find someone to go home with." The woman's expression pinched in a way that said that was as far as she'd go on that subject. Then she sighed, "I didn't take her for the type. She certainly wasn't dressed up for that what with that dress she was wearing."

"I'm not sure I understand. What kind of dress?"

"Well, kind of old fashioned, like prudish, only in a good way." The woman wrung her hands. "What made me worry though was that she left without her phone. That hardly ever happens. People are so attached to those blasted things these days."

Luke took the garment from her and checked the pockets. He pulled out a cell phone.

"Password protected." She lowered her voice to a whisper though Luke was pretty sure they were alone. "We aren't supposed to involve ourselves in case, you know, they meant to not be found for the night, but I tried anyway." The way she pursed her lips after she'd said it gave Luke the impression she either didn't agree with the policy or didn't like having to admit that it happened.

He clicked on the home screen, but she was right. He needed a password he didn't have and didn't have time to figure out.

A scream echoed from somewhere inside the building.

Luke dropped the phone and coat, presenting his sidearm with the fluidity that came from long hours of life-saving repetition as he swept past the woman. He moved through the industrial-size kitchen, senses alert. The woman followed so close behind him he thought she might push him aside.

"Who else is in the building?" he asked.

"Just Zena. That was her that screamed."

Luke scanned both directions before stepping through the interior door. "Wait here."

He had only taken a couple of steps when a petite girl careened around the corner. He swung the gun up. "Stop. Hands where I can see them."

She bounced back a step, eyes wide. "Miss Martha!"

The older woman hurried to stand beside him. "It's Zena. Don't shoot her."

"Miss Martha! There's a woman in the supply closet. I'm about traumatized half to death." The girl pressed her hand over her chest and doubled over, gasping as though she'd just run a mile.

"Good Lord!" Martha gripped Zena's shoulder and forced her upright.

Luke caught the girl's sideways glance at him. His nerves prickled with the impression there was an element of a performance taking place. But that wasn't his primary concern now. He was already in motion when he heard the woman ask the question burning through his brain.

"Is she alive?" Martha's voice quivered when she spoke.

He didn't wait for an answer.

Chapter Seven

E verleigh's head banged against the metal shelving.
Where was she?

The cobwebs cleared in slow-motion as she pushed herself to a seated position. Had someone screamed or had she only dreamed it, adding to the nightmare already tormenting her?

She looked around. Not a nightmare. Real life.

Maybe the scream had been a dream. Or maybe it had been her own terrified voice that woke her. She listened. Silence.

Her fingers wrapped around the can of disinfectant she'd found last night. Her heart thumped against her sternum. She rose and stepped silently to the door. She'd checked it so many times last night the knob was shiny. She tried again.

It turned in her palm. The wave of relief that soaked her quickly gave way to the sting of fear. It might be a trap.

She wouldn't wait around for whoever locked her in the closet to return for another round of whatever twisted game they wanted to play. Ignoring the apprehension making her limbs tingle, she eased the door open enough to peer out.

Armed with the aerosol spray in one hand and her shoes in the other, she slipped barefoot down the carpeted hall. She needed to find a phone. Hers was probably still locked in the coat check closet.

She checked behind her to see if anyone was following her.

"Stop! Show me your hands."

She spun to see the silhouette of a man. Even in the dim light she recognized the gun aiming at her.

"Everleigh?"

"Luke?"

The overhead lights blinked on and the woman from the coat check peeked from behind him.

"That's her." A girl with turquoise hair and a nose ring bobbed from behind them both to point at Everleigh.

Luke lowered his gun, his gaze scanning first her, and then the hallway beyond, then back to her. "Is anyone else here?"

Everleigh shook her head, not sure she trusted her vocal cords to keep the fear she'd felt a secret.

"You can put down the pine-scented disinfectant now." Luke holstered his gun while he spoke.

The can slipped from her fingers and rolled away on the carpeted floor.

"What happened? Are you hurt?" He stepped closer, the concern in his tone making her legs feel shakier than they already were.

A clump of emotion clogged her throat, and she swallowed hard before she could answer. "Someone locked me in the closet." Now that she was finally out and safe, the full measure of the situation rained down on her. Tears stung her eyes.

"That's a lie. The door wasn't locked."

Everleigh looked at the girl now staring at her with defiance. Luke's attention bounced between them, skepticism replacing concern on his face.

"She's right," the older woman said. "We lost the keys about a month ago. The boss hasn't wanted to spend the money replacing the lock since the room is only used for cleaning supplies. It can't be locked from the inside or the outside."

Everleigh sensed Luke's trust turning like a riptide, pulling him into an ocean of doubt.

Pride stiffened her spine. It didn't dry her tears but sent them racing back inside where she could store them up for later. She tugged at her dress, wiggling just enough to adjust it where it restricted her growing indignation. "I assure you I did not spend the night in the janitor's closet for the fun of it. The door was most definitely locked." She crossed her arms over her chest but stopped short of stomping her foot like a petulant child.

"Are you certain it wasn't just stuck? It's possible you were mistaken. It happens." The uncertainty in his expression amped up the questioning tone of his voice.

"Really? You know people who imagine they're locked in a cleaning closet all night on a regular basis?" She wouldn't tolerate being doubted. She'd endured enough of that this past year.

Luke's expression hardened as though he were used to dealing with obstinate people. And knew he'd win if push came to you-have-the-right-to-remain-silent shove.

"Uh . . . " he addressed the young girl.

"Zena," she said as if reading his mind.

"Would you mind getting some water for Everleigh, please?" He gave her a solicitous smile.

The expression she wore said she would mind a great deal.

Everleigh wondered if it would be wise to drink the water once she returned with it.

"I'll go with her," Martha said. "She's liable to wander off and forget."

Once they were gone, Luke stepped close enough she could smell the soap scent still clinging to his skin. He rested a hand on her shoulder and studied her with an intensity that made her squirm. "Are you okay?"

She nodded, denying the tears trying to surface once again at his show of concern.

"Were you drinking last night?"

And just like that the tears were gone. She dropped her shoes to the floor and slipped her feet into the flats, collecting her thoughts and reining in her passions. "Yes. I think I was on my fourth or fifth glass." Which when she thought about it really was how she ended up in the closet.

One look at Luke's expression made her rethink her answer.

"Of water," she clarified, her words sharp.

Luke exhaled, the sound heavy with frustration. "Why don't you tell me how you ended up in a closet then?"

"I didn't want to be at the party. I wasn't in the mood for socializing." She aimed a pointed look at him. His brow lifted in a *what's-new?* expression.

Ignoring him, she continued. "I was looking at the paintings in the hallway when I heard someone—a woman—say *I'm lost*. Then she started crying. It reminded me of my grandmother when she got dementia. I went to check on her and that's when someone locked me in the closet."

Admitting she'd been tricked made the words taste rotten in her mouth.

"You didn't think to go tell one of the staff instead?" Maybe he didn't mean to sound accusatory, but Everleigh wouldn't waste her efforts deciding just how he meant it. Luke Douglas might not realize it, but he was dangerously close to being classified as an enemy. Until she had coffee and something to eat, he'd do well to choose his words carefully.

"No one mentioned anyone being lost last night." Martha returned with a glass of water, her statement casting Everleigh in an even worse light despite the sympathy that laced her speech.

Luke turned his attention to the woman. "Martha, who would've had access to the keys when they went missing?"

The woman's face wrinkled in thought. "Just about all the employees. We kept them on a hook in the office. You can never tell who's going to need to clean up a spill or get a room ready at the last minute."

Everleigh stared at the cup in her hand. At one time her first thought would have been a random attack, nothing personal.

But Justin had been here. She should have left the moment he arrived. Then what? Have him follow her home?

Luke stared at her. The questions she read in his expression weren't encouraging. It was a look she'd become too familiar with. And it was a look that kept her mouth shut instead of sharing her thoughts.

Last night she'd tried to be normal by going to the party, albeit in response to pressure from her friend. Then she'd spent the rest of the night imagining Justin's return and how he might kill her.

She was done.

As soon as the trial was over, she'd call a realtor. It was time to move on. She'd find a new home where she didn't have to watch murderers climbing through windows. Where no one whispered when she walked by or followed her when she drove home from work.

Where no one left sinister letters stuck to her door with butcher knives or locked her in supply closets.

And where it was easier to know who your friends were—her eyes met Luke's—and who they weren't.

Chapter Eight

Zena set a cup of coffee in front of Everleigh then settled in the seat next to her. "So you think someone was going to kill you?"

Everleigh frowned. "That's quite a question to ask." She picked up the coffee and inhaled. No need to take a sip. The aroma and the warmth relaxed her as much as possible under the circumstances. "I think if that had been the intention, we wouldn't be having this conversation now, would we?"

Luke wouldn't let her drive herself home, so she waited here in the small kitchen office for him to finish whatever he was doing. He had a quality about him that made her feel safe. Highly annoyed, but safe. Though he might be skeptical of her story, there was an air of unwavering fairness about him, as if he felt it his duty to protect.

She turned her attention back to Zena. Up close she looked older than Everleigh had first thought. Maybe early twenties. Twenty something troubled years if the look in her eyes revealed anything.

Everleigh sipped the coffee then cringed at the bitter taste that assaulted her tastebuds. "Are you absolutely certain the door wasn't locked this morning?"

"I know a locked door when I see one."

Everleigh bit her lip and turned to focus on the brightly colored poinsettia on the windowsill. The world beyond the glass was cast in gray this morning, making the plant's bloodred leaves seem unnecessarily dramatic. She took another sip of coffee and sank back into the chair.

"Zena! Nobody told you it was break time. Leave Miss Greene alone and get the dining hall cleaned so we can set up for brunch." Martha's voice rattled through the kitchen like wind through an array of suspended pots and pans.

"You'd think you save a person's life you could have a moment of gratitude or something," Zena groused under her breath as she stood. She stared at Everleigh with a watchful, expectant expression.

A soft laugh fluttered from Everleigh, the sound more tired than amused. Opening an unlocked—if it really had been unlocked—door hardly qualified as saving someone's life. But she didn't want to be thought of as unappreciative. "Thank you for the coffee and uhmmm, rescuing me from the closet." She lifted the cup and forced more of the bitter liquid down.

Her muscles loosened. Maybe the laugh, as pitiful as it sounded, was therapeutic. Life felt altogether better than it had just minutes ago. The fear of death she'd wrestled with all night seemed a distant mirage against the wave of contentment blanketing her.

With Zena gone, she put her head on the desk and gave in to the drowsiness settling over her.

She awoke to Luke's hand on her shoulder.

Sitting up, she tried to clear the grogginess that fogged her brain. Her blurry vision only made her more confused.

"Nice to see you, Sunshine. Didn't think I was going to get you to wake up there for a second." His words teased. His tone did not.

"I can't believe I fell asleep." Everleigh brushed her hair back from her face. Her thoughts refused to come together.

"What time is it?"

"Almost nine, and I haven't eaten breakfast yet, so let's get going."

Everleigh tried to stand but found the floor beneath her soft—like walking on a rope suspension bridge. In fact, everything around her seemed only vaguely solid.

Luke reached out to steady her.

"My keys? I need my keys." She began patting her dress as if she expected to find a pocket containing the missing keys. "Where's my coat?"

"I have your coat." Displeasure radiated off him in a way that only added to her growing distress.

"I need my keys. They're in my coat pocket." Her words thickened like cream gravy with too much added flour.

"Are you feeling all right?"

She looked up at him. "Not really. Maybe low blood sugar and lack of sleep." She swayed again.

"Sit. I'll be right back." He left her seated once again, returning with a fresh cinnamon roll and another cup of coffee.

She took a tentative sip and smiled. Sugar and creamer were the magic ingredients, effectively covering the bitterness she'd tasted in the first cup.

"Mmmm . . . much better."

Luke sat on the edge of the desk, watching as she ate the gooey, sweet pastry in what felt like slow-motion. What was wrong with her?

She washed the cinnamon roll down with the last of her coffee. Her equilibrium returned as the food filled her.

"Tell me about last night. Who you talked to, what you ate, what you drank, everything that happened."

Everleigh stared at the poinsettia again, her mind clearing by degrees. None of this was any of his business, but would she mind him making it his business? Did she dare tell him exactly what—or in this case, whom—she believed responsible for her overnight stay?

"I talked to Megan and a couple of other people from work. I had two mini quiches from the hors d'oeuvres and about half a gallon of water."

His forehead creased in curiosity.

"I was uncomfortable, and the nervous energy needed to go somewhere." She shrugged and offered him a sheepish smile.

"Uncomfortable why?"

She bit her bottom lip, her gaze darting to the open door. She harbored a moment of indecision over how much to tell him. "I'm just not a person who enjoys these sorts of events."

That much was true, even if the guest list didn't include a suspected murderer to whom she was the key eyewitness.

"You're sure water is all you had? Someone could have tampered with your drink when you weren't looking."

"You think I'm too naive to know better than to leave my drink unattended?" Her tone was tart. It was the second time he'd implied she'd gotten drunk and slept it off in the closet.

She stood, less wobbly this time, and turned for the door only to have her progress stopped once again by his hand on her arm.

"I'm not trying to make myself an enemy here. I'm just trying to understand how you ended up trapped overnight in an unlocked closet."

"Because it wasn't an unlocked closet. Zena must be lying."

"Even though Martha confirms her story? What reason would they have?"

"How should I know?" she snapped. She exhaled, regretting the sharpness of her reply.

On the one hand, he made sense. She'd probably draw the same conclusion—if she didn't know for a fact the door had been locked. She looked into his face—a face that reminded her too much of Charlie. And right now, one etched with doubt.

Sticking to her story—insisting she knew what she knew—had destroyed the last year of her life. The less she said now, the better.

Chapter Nine

L uke searched her house with the thoroughness of a seasoned operative.

He looked at the tree with the box full of ornaments still sitting on the floor beside it, then he shook his head and made a *tsking* sound as he continued through her house.

Everleigh frowned. He'd never said exactly what he did for a living, and Charlie had never mentioned it. She had the impression this wasn't the first time he'd cleared a house.

He didn't handle it as though he'd learned from watching cop shows or playing video games. The fluid, efficient way he moved through the rooms said there was more to him than he let on.

She grabbed a throw blanket from the sofa and headed to the refuge of her kitchen. Pulling the blanket around her shoulders, she warded off the exposed feeling having her house searched, even in a friendly way, gave her. This was her sanctuary, not meant for anyone else's eyes.

Huddled like a hobo in her own kitchen, she sank into a chair and tried to pray but the words wouldn't come. She didn't know how much time had passed before Luke returned.

He leaned against the doorway. "All clear."

She lifted her head from her hands and gave him a half-hearted smile.

"Grandpa will want to see you for himself before he'll believe you're okay. How about dinner at his house tonight? I'll be over at five to get you."

She nodded. Charlie's house had become a safe haven for her. Even with an interloper like Luke present, it offered something more desirable than a dinner alone in this house.

He stopped at the front door as though there were something more he wanted to say. The expression on his face made the steady cadence of her heart skip into a free style Irish dance as his gaze waltzed over her soul.

"I . . . I just wanted you to know I appreciate your choice of the green dress. The red would have been all wrong."

Heat raced up her neck at the understanding he'd given more than casual scrutiny to the things he found in her private space. She'd forgotten about that atrocity still hanging in her closet. Now he was making fun of her.

The feverishness of her anger changed to a blush, deepening with the realization that the look he gave her wasn't meant to tease.

"I like the green." He walked away, leaving her wondering if he'd meant to compliment her. The thought made her bones turn to feathers. If only she could fly away and leave her fears behind.

A half hour later, she stepped from a hot shower looking sunburned, but satisfied to smell like lavender-scented shampoo instead of the cleaning supply closet. Dressed in flannel lounge pants and a sweatshirt, she headed to the couch with her softest blanket. She snuggled in, her attention captured by the still-undecorated tree.

She could either let its life be a loss or adorn it for its final days . . . by loading it down with cheap ornaments made in China. She rolled her eyes. There had to be a deeper meaning to it all.

On the other hand, the tree was quite breathtaking the way it was. She drifted to sleep with Luke's parting words hovering in her thoughts. *Red was wrong.*

EVERLEIGH AWOKE FROM a dreamless sleep feeling rested. But with wakefulness came restlessness.

The door had been locked. Intelligent, competent people did not just imagine that doors were locked.

Why hadn't she told Luke that she'd seen Justin there?

Maybe because she wasn't sure Luke knew who Justin was or why his presence would bother her.

It was because of Charlie, she told herself. Her fearful imaginings would only worry him.

Or maybe the truth was she didn't want to be seen as needing anyone else. Her life and the stability she craved were up to her. Pride was a prickly thing to let go of.

Checking the time, she hurried to change clothes. She was careful to apply only a small measure of makeup. After all, she wasn't trying to attract anyone's attention.

Keep telling yourself that until you believe it.

She ran a comb through her hair. While it wasn't curly, it would never achieve the level of smooth elegance Megan's did. Her friend's hair hung like a silk curtain. Everleigh's more resembled the beaded curtains at the fortune teller's tent.

With a passing glance in the mirror, she shook her head and stomped from the bathroom. She'd never cared about her looks before. She wouldn't start now.

The knock on her door came early.

"Grandpa wanted takeout. He said you'd know what." The brooding look as he greeted her made her pause. He motioned toward his truck. "Ready to show me how much you know about my grandpa that I don't?"

She turned her back to him under the pretext of digging her keys from her purse. She definitely didn't want him to see the smile she couldn't stop. "You sound as though that bothers you," she said, keeping her back to him.

"It does." He sighed. "That's not your fault. I haven't been a very good grandson lately."

"What stopped you?" She stepped out, pulling the door closed behind them. She wouldn't argue with his confession. Still, she measured her tone. She wasn't looking for a fight even though Charlie deserved better.

"Occupational hazard." He looked away, his jaw clenching as though something bothered him.

He walked behind her as she headed to his truck, then ushered her into the seat as though she were an old lady—or a person someone cared for. She'd bet money Charlie would have done the same for Anna. The thought blanketed her in a moment of hope . . . the kind she rarely let herself indulge in.

He climbed into the driver's seat, then with only one arm, backed the truck from the driveway with the ease of someone who didn't find driving stressful.

Unlike Everleigh. The absence of the overwhelming crush of constant traffic was one of her reasons for choosing the small-town life. Even if it offered only small-town success.

Success and stability. She'd thought she found the place for both until last Christmas had shaken her world.

"Charlie's been a great friend. I'm lucky to have him for a neighbor." Everleigh debated telling him some of her concerns about Charlie's recent forgetfulness.

"Not luck, Providence."

Disagreement tugged the corners of her mouth downward though she didn't voice it. If Providence rather than luck controlled the world, then she'd have to believe what happened to Kariss was Providence.

Luke continued, "Grandpa is the smartest man I've ever known. I've always looked up to him, maybe more so now for the way he insists on continuing to live in the same house where he and my grandma lived for forty something years. He really loved her. I'm not even sure that kind of love exists anymore." His features softened at the recollection. "I'd like to believe it might."

"Same." Her response drew a quick glance.

"Most of his old friends who lived around here have either had to move so someone can take care of them ... or died." He worked his jaw as though the thought of Charlie having to be taken care upset him.

Everleigh considered how he would take the news that maybe the day was coming soon when Charlie couldn't stay here alone. Luke couldn't dread that day any more than she did. Charlie said Luke was staying through the New Year. She'd keep her thoughts to herself a little longer, until she knew what kind of grandson Luke really wanted to be. Saying he cared was easy. Showing it through the sacrifices that might be needed would be a much harder thing to do. Hopefully, he'd see for himself that Charlie was changing—and not for the better. "What about my car?"

"Thought we'd head over to get it after supper."

More cars than normal crowded the streets. Christmas was just two days away. She stared out the window. That meant the trial would start in less than a week.

Troubling images she couldn't unsee and didn't want flickered into her thoughts. Kariss, bloodied and unconscious. The throbbing lights from emergency vehicles reflecting off every surface while flakes of snow continued to fall. And crime scene tape draped around the twinkling Christmas lights, a jarring reminder that all was not calm nor bright.

Everleigh shuddered. As she'd stood in the coziness of her kitchen late on Christmas Eve, wrapped in the homey smell of sugar cookies baking in the oven, a soft snow had begun to fall. A Christmas Eve snow in this part of Texas was a rarity that brought a feeling of magic. She'd watched the fat white flakes float in swirls, dancing in and out of the glow of lights. So peaceful. So quiet.

So deceiving.

And while Everleigh stood mesmerized by the beauty, someone was bludgeoning her twenty-year-old neighbor.

Was there anything in this world that evil couldn't touch?

The familiar guilt balled in her chest. The light glancing off something in his hand had been what first caught her attention as he climbed from the bedroom window. Her first thought was a robber.

No one thinks of murder. She learned too late a shift change at the girl's work had caused her to stay behind when her parents left for the holidays. Not fifty feet from where Everleigh hummed "Silent Night" and baked cookies, evil had reared its wicked head in a sickening attack on the night meant for hope.

She'd called to report a burglary, telling the police no one was home.

Then she'd called her neighbor, Deena Workman, to let her know about the possible burglary of her house. That's when she'd learned she was wrong. Kariss was home alone.

She'd raced next door, phone in hand as she dialed 911 again. The unlocked front door opened in her hand.

The metallic smell of blood had assaulted her, replacing the sweet smells from her kitchen with the scent of death. The rest of the night dissolved into a nightmare that obliterated the joy of Christmas forever as far as Everleigh was concerned.

She pressed a hand over her face, blocking out the world around her, trying to rid herself of the memories. And the guilt.

"Something wrong?" Luke's voice pulled her back.

"Just the effects of last night, I guess." She looked out the window as they passed a church. The banner in the yard read *Jesus is the Reason for the Season*.

The words twisted in her heart.

Did she believe that now? Had she ever really?

Last Christmas proved just how much the world needed Him. But where was He when her sweet neighbor was being attacked? Where was He when Kariss lost the baby she carried?

Luke had asked about her faith. Well, it was on life support right now, barely holding on. A part of her wanted to let go. She'd take care of herself without an absent Savior. But letting go wasn't possible. Turning away from the truth didn't make it untrue.

"About last night . . . " Luke cleared his throat then glanced at her as though formulating his approach.

Everleigh folded her arms over her chest. "I graduated magna cum laude with a master's in business accounting. I'm a certified accountant and the highest-ranking junior partner at the biggest accounting firm in this county. I know when a door is locked."

Lines radiated from the corners of his eyes as amusement—the kind that came at her expense—animated his face.

"What?" Everleigh asked, already regretting her outburst. He probably wouldn't be so keen to compliment her on her outfit the next time.

"I was going to ask you about the person you heard crying." His tongue ran along the inside of his cheek. "But now you've got me all distracted with that long list of sexy impressive credentials. If you're trying to flirt with me, it's working."

His look sizzled through her. She considered flinging herself from the moving vehicle.

"I'm not—" she stammered, indignation burning through her. "Accountants do not flirt."

"Maybe they should." He laughed, leaving her to fidget in her humiliation a little longer. "I'm teasing. I haven't had much practice talking to someone so accomplished. Makes a poor uneducated guy like me all nervous."

"You're making fun of me."

He took his attention off the road and leaned toward her. "I am and I apologize." He turned back to the front. "But you are kind of cute when you get wound up."

"Which is your way of saying you find my emotions amusing and me unattractive most of the time."

"Oh, that is definitely not what I'm saying." His jaw set as though he were steeling himself against something he didn't want to discuss. "Let's stick to the topic at hand for now though. I was going to ask if you'd recognize the voice you heard last night?"

"I don't know." She exhaled. "And I apologize for the unnecessary review of my résumé. I've been asked to second guess myself a lot this past year. I'm not going there again."

"Understandable." He tapped his thumbs on the steering wheel.

"Did Charlie tell you?"

"I know enough." He glanced at her again. "You know they're just doing their job. They have to make their case solid. They can't risk having any surprises."

"I know. I just wish it didn't come with trying to make me sound . . . incompetent."

"Well, you did just spend the night in an unlocked closet."

She snapped her head around to find him looking pleased. He winked, mischief sparking in his eyes.

Shoulders she hadn't known were tight, slipped down and she slouched lower in the seat. While everyone else—other than Charlie—had seemed guarded around her for the past year, Luke Douglas was the first one brave enough to tease her. The hardness in her softened. "Not funny."

"I disagree. I enjoyed it quite a bit." He maneuvered the truck around a corner. "I want to ask you something a bit more serious, though." A hint of hesitation laced his words. "Did you take anything last night or this morning after we found you?"

"Are you asking me again if I was doing drugs?" She couldn't stop the flintlike quality of her words.

"Could have been a prescription med."

"So you don't risk having a case that isn't solid, no. I don't do drugs and I haven't taken any meds of any kind."

"Okay." He reached into his pocket to pull out an empty pill bottle. "I found this in your coat."

"First of all, what were you doing going through my things? And second, it's not mine."

"After I woke you up in Martha's office, you appeared to be . . . medicated. And you're the one who told me your keys were in the coat. I didn't go there looking for drugs."

"It's not mine." She sighed, the fight draining from her.

"I know."

"You know?"

"Yes. I just needed to hear you say it. I had it checked for prints. It's clean. Normal people don't wipe the prints off things they keep in their pockets."

"What is it with you and checking for fingerprints?" Another thought popped into her head. "The police should check for prints on the doorknob."

"Already have. The only prints are yours on the inside and Zena's on the outside. Since she's the one that opened it this morning, that makes sense." The expression he wore said he didn't like having to admit this. "Same as the knife from your front door. The only prints are yours."

Everleigh's fingers dug into the edge of her seat.

"That's not possible. You were there. You know I didn't touch it." The uncertainty she heard in her tone left her shaken. She wouldn't doubt her sanity.

Could she trust Luke? How did he always have the wrong answers for her when he mentioned fingerprints?

Hadn't all this started when he showed up?

Chapter Ten

Luke hadn't decided when or how he would tell her what he'd discovered. Maybe this wasn't the best time, but with the trial so close, there wasn't time to spare.

He'd learned to trust his gut on a lot of things. The last time he'd ignored the feeling, he'd ended up with a 9mm slug in his shoulder.

Something wasn't adding up.

He glanced at the statue-like woman beside him, her hands gripping the seat cushion, the rise and fall of her chest the only movement he detected. Was this witness intimidation? Or was it a potential suspect falling apart under the strain of a guilty conscience?

The signs of drug use in Everleigh this morning didn't help. Some of it might have been written off to the effects of a long and stressful night, but not the slurred speech or dilated pupils he'd seen when he woke her up in Martha's office. His search of her house when he brought her home hadn't been just for her safety. He'd needed to satisfy his curiosity as a neighbor and the grandson of someone who trusted her. Nothing more.

Other than the wiped-clean pill bottle in her coat pocket, he'd found nothing. That lined up with his hunch someone had slipped her something after she'd been found. And he had a hunch that someone was Zena. But why?

Having only Everleigh's prints on the knife was another concern altogether. One not easily explained.

Still, he wanted to believe her.

He looked at her again, secretly hoping for a supernatural revelation one way or the other. His heart was still too tender to expose it to more pain. Not to mention he had an oath to honor as a public servant.

His impression was that she was sincere. Maybe a touch prideful, but not the kind of crazy that would stage her own harassment. Especially since she seemed determined to chalk the threatening notes up to pranksters.

The incident last night had rattled her though.

"What else can you tell me about last night? Did anyone see you leave the party or notice you in the hallway?"

She stared straight ahead, her jaw set, lips pressed in a thin line of fragile resolve. Anger radiated off her like static electricity, ready to zap the next thing she touched. "Why are you so interested? It doesn't really concern you."

"Okay, then who would you talk to? I can drive you over to the station and find one of the detectives or you can call the DA."

"So they could respond the same way you did, by making me think I'm just some attention-starved female who decided it'd be fun to pretend she was locked in a closet all night? No thanks."

"I'm not asking you. I'm telling you to let someone know what happened."

"I did. I told you." She looked out the window as she spoke.

"Yeah, but you haven't told me everything."

No response.

He exhaled and reached into his shirt collar to pull out the chain on which his badge hung. Once he told her who he really was—what he really does—the fleeting chance to hold her heart in his hands would disappear like a mist. The motion drew her attention. The realization drew her frown.

He let her take in the badge for a moment, then tucked it back in his shirt.

"Am I—Are you–" Everleigh stuttered.

"Relax. I'm not on duty," he motioned to the arm still in the sling. "I'm still on medical leave. None of this is in an official capacity. Just friends looking out for each other. But I do want you to know you can trust me and why."

She softened a little, the way burnt toast might with a dab of butter on it.

"Then you know all about what happened?"

"I know a lot. I was working elsewhere at the time, but yes, I'm aware of most of the details."

He let the silence linger. She was thinking about what he'd just revealed. He wouldn't rush her . . . yet.

"He was there last night." Her words came out flat, a note of defeat pressing into them.

"Who?"

"Justin. He came in right after I did." Everleigh's arms went around her middle. Her shoulders hunched in protection mode. "I should have left right then. Stupid, stupid, stupid."

"You sure it was him?" He chose not to address the horsewhipping she was giving herself, though his heart hurt watching her.

She nodded.

"Did you see him after that?"

This time she shook her head.

"You think he was the one who," Luke cleared his throat and regretted it, knowing she'd take it as a sign of doubt, "locked you in the closet? What about the voice you heard? You said you heard a woman."

He'd planned to have this conversation after dinner. He didn't want to spoil the evening for his grandpa. But he was in the thick middle of it now. Might as well press on.

"Something's going on here. We need to talk about it." He forced the words to fall out softly. He knew how to build rapport with suspects, but she wasn't a suspect, was she?

Could his grandpa's feelings for her and his own attraction be influencing his judgment?

He didn't know, but he definitely needed to do more research on the case. He was either riding around with a witness in grave danger . . . or a sociopath.

Experience with both told him it was the first, but that the latter possibility didn't squash his growing attraction scared him.

EVERLEIGH'S APPETITE for both food and company had fled the scene long before they arrived back at Charlie's with supper in hand. When Luke said they needed to talk, he meant he wanted to ask questions she'd already answered. She wanted to believe it was because he was on her side in more than an occupational responsibility sort of way. But she wasn't that delusional.

Maybe her answers had satisfied him, or maybe he'd gotten bored. Either way, she was thankful when he'd switched the conversation to lighter, less interesting topics like how to lower his income taxes. Subjects Everleigh could sink into and answer almost by rote.

Now she couldn't keep up the charade. She excused herself with a headache after Charlie inquired about her lack of eating for the dozenth time.

"I'll see you home. Charlie can help me get your car later, if you're okay with that?"

She nodded, grateful for the kindness. The last time she'd walked home she'd almost been run over. Company was probably a good thing.

Besides, he had a badge. He could probably do whatever he wanted.

Honestly, the thought of entering her empty house left her uneasy. She couldn't bear the idea of not feeling safe in her own home, but until Justin Wicketts was locked away, she wouldn't feel safe anywhere.

Luke helped her with her coat, his one-armed assistance awkward.

He took her hand, then tucked it into the crook of his arm. He smelled good in a way that made her want to inhale more deeply. The warmth of his body next to hers as they walked side by side stirred something in her. She was thankful the dark hid her face, certain it gave her heart away.

Stupid thoughts, but what she wanted right now was to wrap herself in his embrace. When was the last time she'd let herself be hugged? She hadn't grown up in an emotionally demonstrative family, and this longing surprised her.

She blinked the moisture back into her eyes.

It was foolish. Especially since Luke's attention was only due to his occupation. And if he ever looked into her family background, he'd have to start questioning her sanity. How could he not? Even she was starting to. But something inside her sparked with a hope that he was interested in more than protecting a witness, making sure nothing derailed the trial about to happen. Maybe she was tired of living life alone, driven by nothing more than career success. Maybe she wanted a glimpse of what Charlie had with Anna.

To take her first risk with a man like Luke Douglas would be unwise. A man likely as committed to his career as she was to hers.

"If you don't mind, I'll just take a quick look around before I say goodnight. Charlie will sleep better if I do." It was a troubled, lonesome sort of smile that crossed his face as she stepped aside for him to enter.

She slipped off her coat while he wandered through the rooms, his presence filling her house and her heart with more of the unfamiliar longing.

She waited by the door until he finished.

"Looks good. I checked all the windows again. Everything is locked up tight." He wasn't smiling now. Instead, he fidgeted, almost as if he were afraid to look at her. His gaze lingered on her lips. She watched as dark clouds deepened the color of his eyes, as though some emotion she couldn't fathom stormed within. Again, she was keenly aware of the warmth that radiated off him. Her pulse danced.

His Adam's apple bobbed, then he smiled that same lonesome smile and told her good night.

He had reached the street when she finally closed the door. Her chest burned and she realized she'd been holding her breath.

Had he thought about kissing her? Had he wanted to?

Those questions kept her awake long into the night. A welcome replacement to the questions that had plagued her all day.

These were questions that prompted a future of hope, rather than one of death.

Chapter Eleven

Pale light fingered its way around the curtains, prodding Everleigh from sleep. She sat up and stretched, drawing in a deep breath before climbing out of bed.

"Today will be a better day," she proclaimed, refusing to entertain any other thought on the matter.

Her feet touched the cold floor as she stepped off the Oriental rug beside her bed. She padded across the room to get a glimpse of the full moon, the source of the soft, early morning light pulling her from her slumber. Like a cosmic-size pearl dangling from the heavens, it cast a jeweled beam into her window. The radiance soaked into her soul much the same way Luke's presence had blanketed her in a sense of security.

She pushed aside both panels of the curtain to let the light fill her entire window.

A crimson handprint sent her staggering back. Even with the solid glass between them, it seemed to crush her throat, strangling the cry that couldn't break free.

Blood drained from her head like the jagged lines of red trailing from the handprint to pool at the base of the windowsill.

She jerked the curtain back in place, hiding the grotesque image. Drawing in a ragged breath, she backed away from the window until she pressed against the wall. Her gaze went to the baseball bat leaning in the corner. One solid swing would rid her of the image. The desire to do so radiated down her arms like the fierce energy of a lightning bolt.

Her pulse slowed. Just imagining the act released enough fear and fury to let her breathe again.

Only paint, not blood. Right?

She picked up her phone from the nightstand but hesitated. Every molecule of her being shouted she needed Luke. He would know what to do.

She dialed Charlie's number then made her way slowly down the hall, switching on every light and looking in every corner. She should check the rest of the windows. But she couldn't bring herself to touch the curtains.

Charlie picked up on the fifth ring, and she froze. She hadn't considered what she should say. She didn't want to concern him over what might be just another prank.

Having a hallway and some sheetrock between her and the offending handprint gave her space to think.

"Morning, Charlie. Sorry to bother you this early, but is Luke available?" She tried to sound more relaxed than her jangled nerves felt.

"No darlin'. He left early this morning. Said he was meeting a friend for breakfast, then had a full day of things to do. Won't be back until this evening. We got your car outside and ready for you. Even topped off the gas tank." The hesitation in Charlie's voice said she hadn't done a good job of convincing him nothing was wrong.

"Would you mind if I got Luke's number from you? I have something I need to ask him."

EVERLEIGH HEADED HOME from work with a list of things to delay her arrival and an even longer list of worries. Finally, she stopped at the store for chocolate chips and pancake syrup. She picked up a package of bacon but set it back in the cooler. She preferred the bacon from the meat market on the other side of town, and that was reason enough to make the trip.

She'd spent most of the day once again correcting accounting errors she couldn't believe she'd made. She'd been fortunate last time and caught them herself. This time the client had. To say they were not happy with the disaster created in their payroll was an understatement, and rightfully so. But had she really made those mistakes?

Luke's return call hadn't helped. He'd gone by her house as she requested to look at the window then called to tell her there was nothing there. His words had sent her lunging from her desk chair to swing her office door shut before the near hysteria in her voice traveled through the building. When she insisted he look again, he'd accommodated her by sending a picture and assuring her he'd checked all the windows.

After running every errand she could think of, there was nothing left but to head home—if she even wanted to call it that anymore. She wasn't sure she was safe there—mentally, emotionally, or physically.

Face it, Everleigh. You aren't meant to have a home.

The grocery bags on the passenger floorboard promised her a meal of comfort food. Tonight, she'd have a large stack of chocolate chip pancakes swimming in syrup and a side of not-too-crispy bacon—about half the package should do. Then she'd watch reruns of The Next Great Baker while she snuggled on the sofa beneath her favorite blanket and indulged in her fantasy of owning a bakery.

After she double checked all the closets and windows no less than a hundred times.

LUKE LEANED ON CHARLIE'S front porch with a glass of iced tea, watching the sunset and waiting for Everleigh. He hadn't lied when he told her there was nothing on the window. The truth was there was absolutely *nothing* on the window. It had been cleaned recently, more recently than all the other windows. He didn't like it.

Convinced someone was trying to intimidate or discredit her as a witness, he'd shared his concerns with the detective in charge of the case and requested an extra patrol of the area.

And still he wasn't comfortable with her staying alone at her house. He'd finally broken down and shared his concerns with Charlie before bringing up his idea that Everleigh should stay with him while Luke stayed at her place. Even that solution left him uneasy. He didn't want to bring trouble to Charlie's front door. Especially with his growing concerns over his grandpa's mental state.

No surprise Charlie agreed to the arrangement. That was the easy part. Now he had to convince their independent and borderline-obstinate neighbor.

The one he'd come close to kissing last night. Fool.

When she pulled into her driveway, he set the half-empty glass on the banister and headed over.

She slid from the car and stood silently staring at her house, one hand on the open car door as though it were a barrier between her and the doubts she must have about her home.

With no indication she'd noticed him yet, he cleared his throat to alert her to his presence as he stepped closer. "Long day?"

She started, her hand coming up to press against her chest. "You could say that." She closed the car door before turning to face him.

"Didn't mean to scare you, but I might have some good news, as long as we keep in mind good is a relative term in this situation," he teased, wanting to put her at ease though he knew what he had to offer wasn't much in the way of reassuring her.

She looked at him, more eager than guarded. Her vulnerability wrapped around his heart. Every time he was with her it reached out to claim a little bit more of him. He would earn her trust if it was the last thing he did. Although, if he were planning out last things to do, kissing her was going at the top of the list.

"Could we talk about it inside?" He didn't want to discuss the matter in the middle of the driveway.

She looked around as though noticing the shadows of night occupying the spaces between the security lights scattered around the neighborhood. "Let me grab the groceries."

She darted around the car to the passenger side and pulled the bags from the floorboard.

"Allow me." He took the bags from her hands and followed her inside. A strange feeling—one he couldn't name—settled over him, as if he'd lived this moment before. And he had—in every one of his dreams for his future.

And now he *knew* he was an idiot. No one dreamed of carrying in groceries for the next fifty years of their life. But it had worked for his grandpa. Charlie and Anna had what Luke wanted. And if it took carrying in the groceries to have it, he would.

He shook the feeling aside and headed to the kitchen, depositing the bags on the counter. "Must have been a really long day. Syrup, chocolate chips, and bacon. Looks like the makings of a meal I wouldn't mind being invited to share." He grinned.

"I'm a big believer in comfort food as a panacea for rotten days." She emptied the bags without facing him. "So this good news you have is . . . ?"

Luke leaned against the counter and folded his arms, noting she hadn't taken the hint about supper. Or maybe she had and just didn't want his company. To be honest, his news wasn't really all that good, but she needed to know he didn't believe this was a series of twisted juvenile pranks. "There is no print on the window—"

"Yes! There was. I know what I saw." Everleigh set the plastic syrup bottle on the counter with more force than necessary.

He held his hand up, palm out. He'd learned the hard way not to tell a woman to calm down when she was riled up. "There isn't anything at all on the window because it's been cleaned."

Her eyes narrowed as she processed what he'd said.

"The window where you saw the print has been cleaned more recently than any of the other windows. So, unless it's a habit of yours to clean one window at a time, I think we need to talk about some changes."

Chapter Twelve

Everleigh dropped into the nearest chair, wondering if she dared hope he believed her now about the closet as well.

"What are you saying?" Her words were little more than a whisper. Fear crept in, making her uncertain if she truly wanted to know.

"I'm saying it's time you stop pretending this is some sort of misguided prank by the neighborhood delinquents. Someone is harassing you. You need to take this seriously."

"I just want it to stop." Elbows resting on the table, she lowered her head into her hands. "It is about the trial, isn't it?"

"That would be my first guess, but we should consider some other possibilities as well."

"Such as?" She didn't look up.

"Angry ex-boyfriends?"

She raised her head, a small laugh bubbling out. "No exes, angry or otherwise."

"Good." A pleased glint, bordering on relief, flickered in his eyes. "How about an upset coworker or client?"

She shook her head. She did have an upset client thanks to the payroll errors they'd found. This wouldn't be the path of retaliation they'd take, though. A lawsuit was more likely.

"We need to consider this might be an attempt at witness intimidation."

"Then it is him. Justin Wicketts locked me in the closet. Maybe he planned to hurt me then, but something stopped him. Now he's trying to scare me."

"Something stopped him all right. He didn't lock you in the closet." He drew in a breath and held it before continuing. "And he isn't the one who left that piece of artwork on the window."

Everleigh straightened. "How do you know?"

"Because video shows him leaving the country club about twenty minutes after you saw him. The security guard at the gate reported him to the police as a possible drunk driver. They pulled him over, and when he failed the field sobriety test, he spent the night in the drunk tank." His expression melted into misgiving. "He's been locked up in county ever since."

Everleigh swallowed. She'd never in her life had an enemy. "You're right. Good news is relative to the situation."

He tucked his chin as though uncertain. "I've asked Charlie to let you have the spare room at his house while I stay here."

Her gaze locked with his. He didn't look any more pleased about it than she felt. She nodded, the brief movement replacing the words of agreement she didn't want to say. Deep within her she'd known all along this wasn't just kids playing pranks.

Now she was being run out of her home by some crazed person with an evil agenda. Her one chance at some sort of stability ended in an epic failure.

But if Justin wasn't the one doing these things, then the trial might not be the end of it even if he was found guilty.

Her cell phone rang with a special ringtone. She hesitated. Deena Workman. She pulled the phone from her purse with a sinking premonition. *Please, Lord, not more bad news.*

"Hello."

"Everleigh." The woman's voice choked, her words distorted as though she were crying. "You're not going to believe this. Kariss moved!"

Not more bad news—maybe the best news she'd heard in a long time. The Workmans sold their house after the attack, but Everleigh stayed in touch with them and kept up with Kariss, though lately her hope had grown brittle.

Everleigh jumped to her feet, her words tumbling out. "What happened? What does this mean?"

She looked at Luke, wanting to find him sharing in the excitement, but how could he? He didn't know the Workmans. And he couldn't hear the conversation, anyway.

"We don't know yet. But when the nurse changed the linens on her bed, she flinched. Maybe the process of moving her while changing her sheets caused her pain, and she responded. The doctor said it might be a sign that she is coming out of the coma." Deena sniffed, her words tight with emotion. "Oh Everleigh, it's been almost a year. What a Christmas gift this would be! We'll talk again soon."

Everleigh wiped her wet cheeks and turned to Luke as she ended the call. "Kariss. She moved. They think she might be coming out of the coma."

The dark cloud that swept over his face sobered her.

LUKE EXCUSED HIMSELF while Everleigh packed an overnight bag. He understood she felt betrayed at having to leave her home. A person should feel safe in their own house. But the attack that had occurred next door a year ago had proven that wasn't the way the world worked.

Of course, the investigation of that attack had found no evidence of a forced entry. And the accused was the young woman's boyfriend.

Alone on the porch, he pulled his phone from his pocket and dialed the detective's number. If Kariss woke up, she might be able to identify her attacker. And if she could do that, whoever was trying to intimidate Everleigh might go after her as well.

The conversation was brief, and he hung up as Everleigh stepped on the porch with her overnight bag in hand.

She frowned as though something troubled her. "I should probably change the sheets on the bed so they're fresh since you're staying here." The nervousness in her voice said she wasn't exactly thrilled with the arrangement, as though her private space was being invaded. A pretty accurate description.

"No need. I'll sleep on the couch." He asked God to forgive him for his thoughts that if he were going to sleep in her bed, he'd want her there with him. He'd probably need to take advantage of a cold shower tonight.

He reached down and picked up her bag. "Before we leave, there is one thing I'm hoping you might do for me."

A HALF HOUR LATER, Everleigh lifted the last of the bacon from the pool of grease sizzling in the cast-iron skillet. She set it and the platter of chocolate chip pancakes on the table beside the bottle of syrup and real butter she kept in a special crock. She couldn't deny the smile on his face pleased her. For a moment, life in her house seemed normal again.

She glanced at the still-undecorated Christmas tree in the living room. Almost normal.

Luke poured two large glasses of milk and seated himself like a man about to feast.

"Your bachelor status is showing," Everleigh teased as he hefted three of the pancakes onto his plate.

He didn't bother to look at her. "When something smells this good, I have no intention of denying that I don't enjoy my own cooking." He tipped the syrup over the stack of pancakes until it pooled around the edges of his plate.

"I usually make my own syrup, but . . . "

He looked at her, brow lifted.

"It was a long day." She had almost forgotten how much she enjoyed cooking for others. Seated across the table from Luke reminded her of something missing from her life. Something she'd never actually experienced or witnessed but wanted to believe existed.

Especially when he closed his eyes and leaned back, savoring the bite he'd just popped into his mouth.

"They're only pancakes. I don't think they warrant that much enthusiasm." She couldn't contain the pleased smile that contradicted her words.

"Said by someone who has never eaten my cooking."

"Isn't Charlie cooking for you?"

A troubled expression tugged at his features. "I'm trying not to be too much extra trouble. Besides, his culinary talents seem to be limited to spaghetti and oatmeal."

Everleigh touched her fork to a piece of pancake and scooted it around her plate. "I remember when I first moved in, he brought me spaghetti and a chess pie. He made it all from scratch, and it was delicious."

"Well, he's gone Chef Boyardee on me now. Don't get me wrong. It's not as good as what he used to make, but beggars shouldn't complain. It's just that after having it about five times already, I might like a little change. Especially after he forgot to heat it up last time."

"So you cook dinner for him." Though her words might have sounded hesitant, she made sure her expression made her challenge clear.

"Not quite that ready for a change," he said as he stuffed another forkful of pancake into his mouth. "Trust me when I say you don't want me in your kitchen."

Everleigh felt an unfamiliar warmth sliding over her like honey. He was in her kitchen now, and she liked it just fine. She continued swirling her pancake in the syrup. "Does Charlie seem different to you lately?"

Luke's hands froze, hovering above his next bite. He looked up at her. "How so?"

She fidgeted, swallowing her concern about how Luke might receive what she needed to say. She had Charlie's best interests at heart after all. "More forgetful?"

Luke took another bite, chewing slowly. "Yeah, I didn't want to admit it. But if you've noticed it too, then I guess I need to face the truth that something's going on."

Their shared concern for Charlie sobered the conversation for the rest of the meal as they discussed his condition—and his future. It didn't appear to affect Luke's appetite, however. He snagged the last piece of bacon and offered it to her.

She shook her head, already full and wondering how he could eat that many pancakes and still finish off the bacon.

Not ready to lose this moment, she stood anyway and moved the empty plates to the sink. It wouldn't take long to clean the kitchen. With Luke in the house, she was okay with dragging out her departure. She considered asking him if she could stay here since he planned to sleep on the couch. But even if there was nothing improper going on, it would still give the wrong impression. And she had no doubt the entire neighborhood would know about it.

"Anything I need to know before I spend the night here? Pet snakes on the loose? Hot water heater that makes scary noises, that sort of thing?"

She gave him a blistering look.

He sucked in a breath through his teeth. "Yeah, probably not the best question right now. How about just telling me where I can find a blanket for the couch?"

"The closet in the spare bedroom. Just watch out for the stacked boxes." So far, she hadn't needed a place for company, so the room served as a place to store boxes of things she didn't need.

Drying her hands on the towel, she turned to drape it over the handle of the oven door. A crash, followed by a pained exclamation, came from the back bedroom. She rushed toward the sound, entering the hallway as Luke stepped out of the spare room. He rubbed at his forehead where a small stream of blood trickled from a gash.

"What happened? Are you okay?"

"I'm fine." He reached for the towel she still held and pressed it to the cut above his brow.

"That's a kitchen towel. You're getting blood all over it."

"I'll buy you another one." The peevish look he gave her made her step back. He winced as he headed to the bathroom. "And for the record, you could have warned me there was stuff on top of the blanket."

Everleigh frowned. She couldn't reach the shelf unless she used a stool. She knew for a fact there was nothing stored on top of the blankets. "There's nothing on that shelf but blankets."

"And a soccer trophy." He turned on the faucet, dampened a corner of the towel, and wiped away the blood from his wound. "Or there was anyway."

"I don't have a soccer trophy—or any kind of trophy. They don't give trophies for being a bookworm or a baker." At least not until someone thought up the idea for a televised baking competition. And she'd never lived in one place long enough to even be in the running for an award. "Are you sure you're alright? Do you need to go to the ER for stitches?"

He gave her a look that said he would not be going to the ER. "I'm fine. And if the trophy isn't yours, whose is it?"

"No one's. I mean, there isn't a trophy in there. Maybe it was a book or something."

He leaned close to her. "I know a trophy when I'm hit on the head with one."

Unease tingled through her as she spun and headed to see for herself. Luke followed, her kitchen towel still sopping up the blood oozing from his brow.

She stopped abruptly. The blanket he'd pulled down lay dumped on the floor, and beside it was something she'd never seen before. A twelve-inch-tall trophy.

Luke brushed against her back as he stepped around her.

When she reached for the trophy, he grabbed her arm. "You don't recognize this?"

She shook her head.

"Then don't touch it."

"Why?" she asked, backing away as the answer to her own question solidified in her mind. "Fingerprints?"

Luke nodded as he stood, hands on his hips. Everleigh followed his gaze to the dark red discoloration clinging to the base of the trophy. Surely that wasn't blood. But the rational part of her said it was. And it was too dry and dark to be from Luke's small gash.

The temperature in the room seemed to skyrocket. Her shallow breaths made her lightheaded. She had never passed out before, but she'd also never been stalked by a deranged lunatic.

Luke knelt to examine the object then pulled his phone from his pocket.

She needed fresh air but wasn't sure she could make herself go outside to get it. Still, she needed out of this room. She was halfway down the hall when Luke seized her arm.

"Hold on there. I want you to stay where I can see you." He guided her to her bedroom across the hall and seated her on the edge of the bed.

Anger overtook the fear inside her. Someone was deliberately messing with her. And now others were getting hurt because of it.

He stared at her, the expression he wore unreadable. She hoped it wasn't doubt, but he did say he wanted her to stay where he could see her.

"You gonna be okay?" he asked.

She folded her arms across her middle and rocked back and forth without answering him.

"I need to make a call. Promise me you'll stay put until I'm done."

Everleigh nodded. She doubted she could move if she wanted to.

He hesitated as though he didn't want to leave her.

"I'm fine. Really." She watched him move away, feeling the absence of his presence as though someone had opened a window to let in the winter wind.

With his back to her and his voice low, she couldn't make out the conversation. But the way he glanced at her every so often made her want to find a hole she could hide in. She couldn't stand seeing that questioning look on his face when he turned to her.

The man who'd sat at her kitchen table like a trusted friend. Would he abandon her in pursuit of his job?

Chapter Thirteen

Everleigh sat in the wingback chair she'd bought at an antique store. The chair looked like something that should have been passed down like a family heirloom. Something she'd never have. She hugged a plaid throw pillow against her chest and stared at the bare Christmas tree—anxious and alone.

It hadn't taken long for a squad of officers to descend on her house. Charlie had seen the commotion and started across the street, but Luke spotted him and sent him home.

At least Charlie would have counted as a friend—if his grandson hadn't interfered.

Did Luke trust her? Could she trust him?

A pressure cooker of emotions simmered within her. She alternated between biting the inside of her lip and digging her thumbnail into her palm. She didn't want to cry. Not in front of them.

Not in front of Luke.

One rebellious tear slipped out before she could stop it. She swiped it away.

The discovery of the possible murder weapon in her house couldn't be good. How long before they put handcuffs on her and took her away?

She stood and moved to the bare tree. The crisp, pine scent soothed her. Stooping, she examined the collection of ornaments then removed a small box of brightly colored glass balls. One by one, she hung the shiny decorations on the tree, watching as the light from the ceiling danced across their round bodies. Beauty from ashes.

Maybe all of life existed as a fragile, windswept cinder, blowing where the breath of God took it. And the most important legacy of a person's existence were moments of beauty they created that lingered on in the hearts of others.

She wanted to believe there was no way they could suspect her, but she knew her own skeptical nature. If she were in their shoes, she'd doubt her story too.

Tuning out the noise and activity around her, she lost herself in her task of placing each ball where it would sparkle in the light.

A throat clearing pulled her back. She turned to see Luke watching her, arms folded over his chest, and realized they were alone now.

Was he the one left to arrest her? It was an especially cruel thought.

This wasn't his jurisdiction, though. She didn't know much about the rules, but she was pretty sure that was a critical piece of information.

"You want some coffee, water, something I can get you?" His voice held a note of compassion, but she didn't dare trust it.

Shaking her head, she returned to the tree, placing the last of the ornaments on the soft, green branches. An involuntary sigh confirmed that the decorated tree didn't solve her problems. She planted herself on the couch and rubbed her temples.

The growl of the coffee grinder, followed by water pouring into the tank of the coffee maker carried to her. She never drank coffee at this time of night, but now she regretted refusing his offer.

His voice wafted to her along with the aroma of coffee. He was on his phone. Judging by the conversation, it must be Charlie.

Moments later he reappeared carrying two cups.

"Humor me," he said as he sat one on the end table near her.

"I'm all out of humor." Weariness she had plenty of.

Blood still smeared the side of his face, but the gash had been covered by two butterfly bandages.

He made a sound—half laugh, half exhale—as he sat next to her.

"I don't understand." She picked up the mug, running her finger around the smooth rim.

He cocked his head in her direction without exactly looking at her. "What do you mean?"

"For starters, how did that thing get in my house? I must have left a door unlocked. Stupid, stupid, stupid. And then why didn't the police arrest me?"

He stood, lifted the cup from her hands, set it aside, then pulled her to her feet. "Come with me." Holding her hand with a touch that felt too secure for her to fear him, he led her down the hall, through the utility room, and out the backdoor.

"Did you just lock us outside?" Everleigh couldn't take much more for this day.

"Hold on. You'll see." He pulled a credit card from his pocket, examined the edge, then wedged it between the door and the doorframe. In less than a minute, he had the door open again.

"I always thought that was a myth." Everleigh hugged her arms around her middle.

"Very few doors are built with the latching mechanisms installed properly." He showed her where the hole in the frame failed to match up with the bolt in the lock. "Without a good deadbolt on this door, I suspect it was an easy in for whoever did this."

Everleigh hugged herself tighter. Based on what he had shown her, they could just as easily have entered while she slept. She swayed, her thoughts making her lightheaded. They—whoever they were—had been in her house.

"Come on." He ushered her back inside, steadying her with his uninjured arm.

Seated on the couch once again, Luke wrapped an arm around her shoulders and pulled her to his chest. She resisted for only a moment before his tender strength drew her surrender. She relaxed against him. "And as for why they didn't arrest you, they don't consider you a suspect. From what I can tell, they are treating this as witness tampering. But . . . "

She held her breath, unsure what went with the *but* and equally unsure she wanted to know.

"I'd feel better if you weren't out of my sight for the foreseeable future."

She felt the intensity of his gaze on her.

"Is this because you don't trust me?" She knew that wasn't true. Not after all he'd done for her—all he was doing right now—since the evening had gone haywire. But expectations ingrained since childhood were hard to let go of. The new kid was always eyed with suspicion. And Everleigh was always the new kid.

"I think the question you need to ask is 'Do you trust yourself?'" His fingers toyed with her hair. "Or better yet, do you trust God?"

She moved away. "The God who let all of this happen when He could have stopped it?"

"The God who gave us free will. We chose this, not Him."

Chapter Fourteen

Pounding on the door jerked Everleigh from a fitful sleep. Across the room, Luke dozed in the wingback chair, legs extended across the floor. The last thing she remembered was resting her head on his chest.

"Hey in there," Charlie called from the porch.

She hurried to open the door and let him in, guilt washing over her. While he'd probably spent the night worrying about them, she hadn't given him a thought.

Some friend she was.

Luke raked his fingers through his hair then scrubbed his face as though getting rid of the sleep.

"Is that how you were planning to protect Everleigh? By sleeping?" Charlie sounded cross. Why hadn't Luke sent her to Charlie's house as planned?

Because then he couldn't have watched her himself. Or maybe he didn't want her around his grandpa. Maybe he really didn't trust her.

She swallowed the insecurity that came too easily, reminding herself she wasn't that child anymore.

"Nothing happened." Luke rolled his shoulder then scratched beneath the strap of the sling supporting his other arm. His gaze roamed over her as if verifying the statement he'd just made. The spark that ignited in his eyes burned away the last of the sleep, suggesting he didn't mind her harried appearance this morning.

Her hands went to tangled hair that hung in front of her face, fingers combing through the knots as she tried to smooth the wayward locks.

"I'll make some coffee." She whirled in the direction of the kitchen.

"No need. We already got a pot going. Just came over to fetch you two before Anna's biscuits get cold." Charlie headed out the door while Everleigh and Luke exchanged concerned glances.

They hurried after him. Inside his house, they found a coffee pot filled with oatmeal instead of coffee grounds and a pot of spaghetti on the stove.

"Grandpa, you feel alright?" Luke asked.

"I'm not sure. I just can't remember what I ought to do. Where's Anna? She'll know."

The tears Everleigh had denied last night refused to be contained any longer. She grabbed the coffeepot and went to work trying to rid it of the oatmeal. After scraping the lumps into the trashcan, she attempted to scrub the charred residue from inside the pot. Finally, she gave up. Facing the sink with the ruined appliance still gripped in her hands, she cried, unable to stop the flow of emotions she'd kept sealed up inside of her for months.

Luke came to stand behind her, gently turning her to face him. "You okay?"

Everleigh wanted to reassure him but couldn't.

He pulled her close, maneuvering his injured arm so that she fit beneath the sling.

She hesitated. "I'll hurt your shoulder."

"I'm more bothered by how you're hurting my heart."

She melted into him. This might not be the smartest thing to do, but she lacked the strength to keep pretending she was okay.

And she was tired of being independent. Would it be so bad to take a chance and let someone else help carry the load?

He rubbed her back, but she ended the embrace sooner than her heart wanted. "Charlie?"

"I called his doctor but got the answering service. I'm hoping to hear back soon. Until then, I told him it's your birthday, and we're taking you out for breakfast. It'll be easier to get him to go if that's all he thinks we're doing."

"You lied to your grandpa." Everleigh sniffed as the last of her tears made dark blotches on her shirt.

"I thought it was for a good cause."

"I have to go to work." She swiped her wet cheeks. Should she be concerned Luke would lie to someone he loved? Or was her emotional exhaustion making too much out of it? He was right. Getting Charlie to go without causing a fuss would be best.

"You look spent." He tucked a strand of hair behind her ear, letting his fingers trail a slow path along her neck until they settled on her shoulder. "I know I sure wouldn't want you working on my books today."

She stepped away, reaching for a napkin from the holder on the table, pretending she wanted nothing more than to discreetly wipe her nose. She couldn't tell him about the mess she had at work. A mess that wasn't her doing–no matter how much everything pointed in that direction. Those mistakes she'd found were too big, too obvious. And even though she was the only one that had access to that account, she hadn't been the one to make them. Last night convinced her the game being played here was bigger than she realized.

"There's something else you need to do today." The hesitancy in his words turned her around to face him. It matched the guarded look she saw on his face. "I told the detective you'd come in to answer some more questions today." Once the words were out, he straightened as though anticipating an argument.

"You did what? And why? I told them everything I knew last night." Her fingers curled into fists. The rational part of her recognized the overreaction. But that wasn't the part she was going with right now. "Why didn't you tell me this last night?"

The source of her anger reared its cruel, mocking head. It wasn't that she needed to answer the same questions time and time again. It was that he had intentionally kept it from her. He had no right to do that. She'd grown up in an environment where she never knew where she'd be living at the end of the day. She'd lost count of the times she arrived home after school to find out it wasn't home anymore as her grandmother whisked her off to some place new.

"Would you have rested if I had?" He stared at her, seemingly unfazed by the ire oozing from her being. "It's not a big deal. Just a formality."

"You said I wasn't a suspect."

"You're not, although technically everyone's a suspect until they aren't." Luke's tone softened, as though he might have an ounce of empathy for her. As though maybe he understood.

She sank into a kitchen chair. There. He'd said it. His response to her question about whether he trusted her last night echoed in her head. He hadn't answered the question. He'd redirected it. Well, she had an answer now.

"Sometimes I wonder if truth is what the world really wants."

Chapter Fifteen

Their conversation had been interrupted by the return call from the doctor's office. But Luke wasn't done.

It had taken all morning to accomplish breakfast, Charlie's appointment, and Everleigh's trip to the station.

He glanced at her as he walked beside her. She'd done well with the detective's questions. Patient and thorough. But now she looked done in.

In a move that surprised him as much as it must have her, he took her hand and placed a kiss on the back of it. "You're doing good. We're going to get whoever is behind this." He stopped short of saying *I promise*, because though he meant it, he knew he couldn't guarantee it.

She didn't resist, and he didn't let go. Her gaze said she was a million miles away after their busy morning.

Breakfast had been threaded with a tension that hummed like electricity running through power lines. Fortunately, the trip to the doctor's office revealed that an adjustment of Charlie's medications should correct his recent confusion.

Charlie hadn't said much on the drive home. He'd appeared to be lost in his thoughts as well. Judging by his expression, they were sad thoughts.

Sad thoughts about things that Luke couldn't fix or change. Frustration steeled its way along his shoulders and set his jaw in determination.

A fine job he was doing taking care of them.

He'd settled Charlie down for a nap, making Everleigh wait before he escorted her to her house—where she insisted on going despite his objections.

He glanced at her from the corner of his eye. Maybe he could take away some of the worry he saw there. He opened his mouth to tell her she was safe with him, but she cut him off.

"What's wrong with me?"

Her question torpedoed his plans and left him stymied. What was this about?

She continued without waiting for his response. "You asked me last night if I trusted myself."

He angled his head toward her and rubbed his thumb across her knuckles, hoping he might draw her from her shell to let him protect her . . . body, heart, and soul.

She stopped in the middle of the street. "All my life I've doubted myself. We moved so many times when I was a child, I became a chameleon so I could fit in. I got so good at it I forgot who I was." Her gaze flashed up to his, giving him a brief glimpse into her unguarded soul. "Or maybe I never knew. But having to confront this—having to tell the truth and keep telling it while it feels like no one believes me—it's helped me find myself again."

"Good." Luke made sure the word came out clear and firm. He dropped her hand and brushed his fingertips along her cheek, then slipped them into her hair. He needed her to know he meant it. Cupping her head in his palm, he looked into her eyes. He didn't blink. "I'm on your side, Everleigh."

Her eyes glistened, and she looked away. "You asked me how my faith was the first time we met. The problem is I'm not sure I have any."

When she looked back at him, the raw honesty and fear he saw ripped his heart open.

"I want to. Sometimes I think I almost can. But I just can't reconcile the things that happen with a God who loves."

His emotions warred inside him. He couldn't go down this road again. He liked her with more than a casual interest. Something much more.

Something with the power to leave him broken beyond repair.

Besides, he needed to get this attraction out of his head for professional reasons. If he responded to the desires taking root in his heart, it might be used against the prosecution in the upcoming trial. He couldn't get involved with her now. It baffled him why waiting would seem so hard when all undercover work was about waiting.

Maybe it was because he feared if he waited, he might lose this chance for both of them.

EVERLEIGH STARED AT Luke, horrified by what she'd just shared.

He took her hand again. "How 'bout we continue this conversation somewhere besides the middle of the street?" He led her to the sidewalk as a car drove by.

She pulled her hand away and shoved her hands into her pockets. Squeezing her eyes shut, she forced an end to thoughts of what she'd just admitted. When she opened her eyes again, she stared at Luke's boots, not daring a look at his face. "I'm sorry. I don't know why—"

"Everleigh," he stopped her. "There's nothing wrong with you."

He tipped her chin up, forcing her to look at him. Forcing her to notice that his gaze lingered on her lips.

His phone chirped.

He didn't move. Didn't even blink.

"You should get that. It might be Charlie." She stepped away from what she feared would have been a kiss from which she would never recover. Disappointment flickered across his face, like a thirsty man denied a drink of water. The thought sent fire through her veins. She pressed a hand to her chest, covering the heart he'd just stirred to new life.

His frown shifted to concern as he checked his phone. "It's the doctor's office."

The conversation was brief, but the worried lines that etched his face told her it wasn't good news. He hung up and shoved the phone back into his pocket. "The doctor wants to see Charlie again. Something on his blood test came back abnormal, and they want to check him again before they adjust anymore of his medications. I'll get Charlie in the truck then pick you up."

She crossed an arm over her middle and rubbed her forearm even though she wasn't cold. "I'm going to stay here."

"I don't think that's a good idea."

"I need some time to myself."

He looked across to Charlie's house, sighed, then turned back to her. "Stay inside and keep your phone with you. Call me at the first sign of anything wrong."

She stifled a humorless laugh. It would be easier and less time consuming to tell him if anything seemed right.

Chapter Sixteen

Everleigh understood why Luke didn't want to leave her alone. She could have eased his worry by going with him. She didn't.

After jamming a chair under the doorknobs on both doors, she showered, slipped into an old pair of jeans and a faded flannel shirt she found at the back of the closet. Letting her hair air-dry was a sure sign she was close to giving up.

The television remote was already in her hand when the Bible on the bookshelf caught her attention. She seated herself on the sofa and tried to ignore it.

But she couldn't. She needed an answer, any answer, for the reason her faith was drowning beneath the waves of turmoil surrounding her. Determined to find one, she retrieved the Bible and returned to her seat.

With her cell phone resting on the cushion beside her, she curled her legs beneath her and opened the long-neglected book.

The words from the church sign she'd seen the other night captured her thoughts. *Jesus is the Reason.*

Jesus is . . .

She'd come to a crossroad where she had to decide. Jesus is . . . what?

Opening to the Gospel of Matthew, she read. The words were familiar, but they took on a new substance, something real she could hold onto if she tried. When she came to the story of Peter walking on water she stopped, paralyzed by the words on the page. Like Peter, she'd taken her eyes off Jesus. She'd seen only the blood and the grief and the injustice—the waves and the storm and the dark depth beneath her.

"And immediately Jesus stretched out His hand and caught him, and said to him, 'O you of little faith, why did you doubt?'"

She read the verse again, repeating it out loud, lingering over the words that reminded her Jesus was right there, ready to catch her.

A weight she didn't know she'd been struggling under seemed to slip away as she let go of herself—her desperate longing for stability and respect—and fell into the arms of Christ.

Lost in her rediscovery of God's Word, time slipped away until someone banged on her door.

"It's Megan. I have to talk to you."

Everleigh opened the door to find her normally polished friend in such a state of dishevelment it caused her to step back. The tear-stained cheeks and red-rimmed eyes were out of place on her coworker.

Megan sagged against her. "I'm sorry. I'm so sorry," she babbled, repeating the words over and over.

Everleigh staggered under the unexpected weight. She untangled herself and took hold of Megan's arms, squeezing them to stop her incoherent rambling.

"It's my fault." Megan hiccupped. "I shouldn't have done it, but I got caught up in it, then I was afraid. I really needed the money. I didn't mean for you to get hurt."

"Slow down. You aren't making any sense." Everleigh pulled her friend inside. She scanned the street before closing and locking the door. "What's wrong?"

"Everything." Megan sank onto the sofa, her hands clasped between her knees, noticeably avoiding eye contact.

"I'm really not a bad person—I promise I'm not. But I have to tell you I did something bad. Really bad. And I don't have any right to ask you to forgive me. I hope you will, but I'll understand if you won't."

Megan's words gushed out. "You weren't supposed to get hurt. I never would've agreed to that, I promise."

Unease knotted in Everleigh's stomach. "What are you talking about?"

"Everything. I helped her do it all."

"Do what? Who are you talking about?" A cold edge crept into Everleigh's voice.

A long pause followed as Megan sniffed. "Trudy Wicketts."

The implications of Megan's confession slammed into her as though she'd been punched. Justin Wicketts's mother. She reached for the chair, bracing herself to keep from shaking.

"Please understand. She was my Sunday school teacher. I looked up to her. She was always so . . . perfect. I wanted to *be* her when I grew up." Megan shot to her feet, pacing as though she could outmaneuver her guilt. "I found out it's not as easy as she made it look. I started spending money on expensive things to cover over the imperfections—so people would see the things and not me." She toyed with the diamond bracelet she wore, twisting it around her wrist. Dropping her arm to her side as though the bracelet burned her skin, she moved to the Christmas tree and placed her finger on a silver ornament.

Everleigh watched her friend—if she could even be called that anymore—wrestling with her shame as she continued touching the ornaments one by one. She didn't have the words to comfort Megan. She wasn't sure she'd use them if she did.

"I'm in a lot of debt." The ornaments bobbed as Megan's fingers brushed against them. The movement distorted her reflection, but it also made the tree appear to sparkle as the colored balls caught the light and cast it back at unexpected angles. The tree seemed to be dancing in a soft breeze.

Mesmerized by the moment, Everleigh was captured by a new thought.

Like the bobbing ornaments, a once perfect world had been disturbed by a single touch. But even in the disturbance, light still found a way to create beauty.

Megan's voice broke the spell. "All she wanted the first time was the knife. I had to arrange for you to be the one to wash it so your fingerprints would be on it. But it was Trudy, and I knew she'd never hurt you. I thought it seemed a bit odd, but it didn't seem, you know, dangerous. And they were about to repo my car. That one covered the payment."

Megan looked at Everleigh. "Stupid of me, right? But I needed the money. I couldn't let people find out I was really broke."

"What else?" Everleigh's voice wasn't exactly cold, but neither was it filled with compassion.

"The door. I picked you up so I could leave the back door unlocked. Trudy said she wanted to see for herself the view out your kitchen window. Like how sure could you be that it was Justin you saw? I understood a mom wanting to defend her son. I didn't believe she'd do anything wrong." She swallowed. "She told me about the trophy later."

"And the Christmas party?"

"I had to get you there and make sure you saw Justin."

"Are you the one who locked me in the closet?"

"No. That was Zena. I didn't even know about that until the next day. I just assumed you'd left without saying goodbye. I think she was supposed to drug you at the party." Megan rubbed her hands as though trying to rid them of something that wouldn't let go. "The mistakes in your clients' accounts . . . I did that. I didn't want to, but she said she'd tell everyone what I'd done if I didn't. I couldn't stand the thought of everyone knowing the truth. You don't understand how hard it is when you're supposed to be this great success but you're just a failure."

"And a coward?"

Megan's gaze met Everleigh's.

"That too. Until today. All this time I've watched you be brave, telling the truth and sticking with it though it could cost you everything."

She inhaled a shaky breath, taking a tentative step toward Everleigh. "I'm sorry. I never meant for you to get hurt. I was only thinking about me."

"What changed?" Everleigh wasn't sure she cared, but she needed time to process what she'd heard.

"A dream."

"A dream?"

"There was a storm, like at sea, and I was drowning. But you were there, and you weren't drowning. It was like you had this gift for just floating on the same waves that pulled me under. The sea was like the truth, but the waves were the lies and deceptions. I couldn't get above them to where you were. When I woke up, I did something I haven't done in a long time. I opened my Bible and prayed."

Everleigh looked at her own Bible lying open on the sofa.

"Isaiah 57:20 . . . 'But the wicked are like the troubled sea, when it cannot rest, whose waters cast up mire and dirt.' That's how I felt. Like I'm this filthy water splashing yuck on everyone around me." Megan reached for her then dropped her hand back to her side when Everleigh stiffened. "I don't want to be the filthy water that makes everything around me ugly."

Everleigh stared out the window. What could she say after all her friend had confessed today? She might not have gone as far as Megan to deceive—she hadn't needed to—but they'd both been fakes. She faced her friend, but still couldn't find the words.

Megan folded her arms across her chest, each hand rubbing the forearm beneath it. "Trudy's not right. There's something off. Like how she visits Kariss all the time."

Everleigh frowned. "What did you say?"

"I said I think it's wrong she visits Kariss. She takes her flowers nearly every week. She even buys the Workmans gifts like tickets to the Christmas cantata today. It all looks nice, but it feels wrong somehow."

"Why would they let her near their daughter when her son is the one accused of trying to kill her?" Everleigh's voice pinched to the point of sounding shrill even to her own ears.

"Trudy's father, Pastor Stanmore, was like royalty around here."

Everleigh's intuition spun. "Where is Trudy now?"

"She's headed to the Brookstone facility with some Christmas gifts. She wants to surprise the Workmans when they get back." Megan grasped at Everleigh's arm. "Please don't tell anyone what I've done. Promise me you won't."

Everleigh broke free, staring at Megan as though she were someone she'd never met. Then she snatched her phone from the sofa and found her purse. "I have to go."

Chapter Seventeen

E verleigh pressed her foot to the accelerator. Her fingers were white around the steering wheel as she zipped in and out of traffic on the interstate. Her prayers tumbled out like a bag of garage sale bargains—random, disjointed, and often tattered.

Luke didn't answer his phone. The message saying she'd reached his voicemail stabbed her with betrayal. He'd said to call if she needed anything.

I guess he never said he'd answer if I did.

Next, she called Deena Workman and listened to another voicemail greeting.

She spotted Trudy Wicketts's familiar SUV ahead and sped up. A pickup truck to her left decided to take the next exit, cutting her off and causing her to slam on the brakes. Her cell phone skidded and dropped between the seats.

An eighteen-wheeler blocked her as she tried to go left. Trudy's vehicle was nowhere in sight when she finally reached the exit.

The hospital district was minutes away. A couple of blocks' worth of traffic regulated by one-way streets and traffic lights on every corner. Not to mention pedestrians on their cellphones, heads down, oblivious to the world around them.

Her tires squealed as she swung into the parking garage and stomped on the brakes to wait for the arm to lift. She snatched the ticket then whipped into the first open spot she saw, ignoring the *Reserved for Dr. Goshorn* sign.

The elevator light blinked higher as she raced toward the doors. She wouldn't wait.

Taking the stairs, she headed toward the third floor to the walking bridge that connected the parking garage to a large bank of elevators.

A temporary gate covered in a blue trap and an *Out of Order* sign stopped her when she stepped out of the stairwell.

Unless she waited for the parking garage elevator to make its return trip, the stairs were her only option. She took the steps two at time until her thighs felt like burning coals.

Fighting to catch her breath, she clutched at the sharp pain in her side as she left the stairwell. She looked for a nurse, but the station was empty.

Kariss's room was at the far corner of the last hall. Her parents had been thrilled when they'd moved her to a room with better views, not that she noticed.

Fear propelled Everleigh the length of the hall in strides just short of running. Heart still pounding from exertion, she pushed through the heavy door to find Trudy standing beside Kariss, a bottle and syringe in her gloved hands.

"What're you doing?"

Trudy smiled and drew the plunger back on the syringe. "Putting late-night television to good use. It's amazing all the helpful things you can learn from those horrid shows."

Everleigh shifted, attempting to draw her away from Kariss. If she could reach the call button, she might get help, but she couldn't take her eyes off Trudy.

The woman tossed the bottle to her. Without thinking, she caught it. The brief distraction gave Trudy a chance to move closer to Kariss, near enough to inject her with whatever she had in the syringe.

Everleigh dropped the bottle and lunged for the woman. Grabbing Trudy, she jerked her away from Kariss. Trudy jabbed the needle into Everleigh's arm instead. She slammed the plunger forward, depositing the full contents into Everleigh's burning muscle.

She opened her mouth to scream but Trudy's palm connected with her cheek. Her head snapped to the side. When she looked back, Trudy stood over Kariss, the needle of the now-empty syringe hovering near the clear tubing feeding the contents of an IV bag into Kariss.

"Let's not draw attention by raising our voices. Have a seat so I don't get nervous and accidentally stab this into one of these plastic tubes. If I understand correctly, getting air into them is bad, very bad."

Everleigh's breath still came in labored snatches, her pulse racing. Whatever Trudy had injected into her, she needed to slow her breathing and keep her head. She eased down into the chair. "You won't kill her. You can't get away with it."

"Hmmm . . . I came so close to succeeding the first time. Thanks to you, I think I really could pull it off this time." She cocked her head and stared at Everleigh. "Just sit there and be a good girl. This will be over soon."

Everleigh forced her rising panic aside. The lines between reality and nightmare were blurring. Her limbs felt weak from the hard run up the stairs, but she had to hold herself together. Maybe if she kept Trudy talking. "It was you. You tried to kill Kariss?"

"Mm-hmm."

"Why? Why would you do that then let your son take the blame?" The fluttering sensation in her heart now felt different from the racing pulse caused by her exertion.

"She wouldn't listen to reason. I hope that won't be an issue for you as well." She pursed her lips before continuing. "Justin wasn't supposed to be blamed. He went there to protect me. Silly me. I left the weapon at the scene. He had to get the trophy out of there before anyone discovered her—or it. Don't you know good girls aren't up staring out their windows at that time of night?"

"What kind of monster are you," Everleigh squeezed her hands into fists as though she could hold onto consciousness despite the strange dizziness creeping over her, "that you would let your son take the blame for a murder you committed?"

"There won't be a trial, not for him. You've become such an unstable witness." She tilted her head. "Soon to be a dead one. By the way, have you been saved? If not, we should pray right now. I wouldn't feel right about letting you die without at least saying the sinner's prayer with you."

Darkness inched its way around the edges of Everleigh's world. She was going under. She tried to stand, but she wobbled in a room that now spun like a tilt-o-whirl. A vague awareness of Trudy's movements registered.

The woman placed something in her hand, but she was too confused to understand what, and too weak to resist. Her skin felt damp, perspiration beading on her forehead and upper lip.

From somewhere down the hall an alarm sounded.

Trudy stooped down in front of her. "Do you know what my favorite Christmas carol is? "Silent Night." Thank you, Everleigh, for this Christmas gift." The woman straightened and reached for the door, pausing one more time before opening it. "Looks like all is calm, all is bright once again."

Chapter Eighteen

L uke ripped off his sling, freeing both his arms. He could handle the possibility of tearing open the incision, but he couldn't handle the possibility he'd fail Everleigh because he had one arm bound up in that stupid thing. He winced, then gritted his teeth, as he straightened the newly freed arm. He tossed the empty sling in the trash can as he sprinted past.

He'd dropped his grandpa off at his house after the second trip to the doctor's office, then run to pick up his new prescriptions. How could everything have fallen apart in such a short amount of time?

A sense of foreboding had him about to jump out of his skin. Luke was sure he could've pried the elevator doors apart with his bare hands. When he'd seen a missed call from Everleigh, unease had toyed with him. When she hadn't answered his return call, the unease gave way to full blown concern. As much as he had hated to, he'd called Charlie.

Learning Everleigh's car was missing from her driveway had sent Luke into all-out-guardian mode. Unfortunately, he'd had nothing to point him the right direction until Charlie called back and put a crying Megan Lively on the phone.

Charlie had found her crying on Everleigh's porch. He didn't understand half of what she said through the sobbing and broken sentences. But she'd been clear she believed Everleigh was headed to Brookstone to see Kariss.

Megan had clammed up when he asked her why. There was only one reason he could imagine. She must have thought Kariss was in danger. He had a hunch Megan knew more than she was saying, but Luke didn't have time to drag the truth from her.

The elevator doors opened, and he lurched forward, almost knocking over a woman equally in a hurry to exit. "Pardon me." He slid to the side as she stepped out. She barely glanced at him before hurrying on. The woman looked vaguely familiar, but now wasn't the time to ponder old acquaintances.

Chaos greeted him when the doors opened to the eighth floor. A couple of nurses rushed past him wheeling a crash cart toward the commotion. He followed them, his stomach sinking as instinct told him it was Everleigh.

No one looked up when he stepped into the room packed with medical personnel. Two nurses were tending to an individual in the hospital bed while two more bent over a shaking body.

Luke froze. Everleigh.

Stiff and jerking, she thrashed unconscious on the floor. Luke dropped beside her and helped them roll Everleigh to her side.

"What happened?" he asked.

"You tell us and we'll both know." The older nurse's words were clipped as she tore open the package she held and removed a prefilled syringe from it. "Do you know this woman?"

"Yes." He cradled her head gently, careful not to restrain her while trying to keep her from hitting it against the floor. "Everleigh, can you hear me? Hang in there. Don't give up. Charlie needs you." Emotion choked his throat. "I need you."

The nurse gave him a scrutinizing look before returning her full attention to Everleigh. She slipped the syringe into Everleigh's mouth. "Buccal midazolam should calm the seizure. Does she have a history of seizures?"

"I don't know." Luke hated the admission. He wanted to know everything there was to know about Everleigh—and not just so he could answer the nurse's questions.

"Her pulse is faint and dropping." One of the nurses pressed two fingers against Everleigh's wrist. The calmness in her voice belied the urgency in her face.

"Where's the gurney? We need to get her to ER."

Luke shifted. He was prepared to scoop her up and carry her if need be. Something caught his eye from beneath the bed, and he reached for it. Confusion muddled his thoughts as he looked at the label on the medicine bottle in his hand. He turned to the nurses. "Insulin. She's reacting to an insulin overdose."

He'd been called to a similar scene while on duty his first year of patrol. A teenager had used his sister's insulin to commit suicide. The kid had passed away while Luke performed CPR. The memory turned him cold.

That wasn't going to happen to Everleigh. They were in the hospital. They couldn't let her die.

The nurse snatched the bottle from his hand and checked. "Get a blood sugar reading. Who's Charlie Douglas?"

"He's my grandpa," Luke said, hating where his thoughts took him at the sight of Charlie's insulin bottle.

"Do you know if she's suicidal?"

Luke could only shake his head. He knew so little about this woman.

A nurse swabbed the tip of Everleigh's finger with alcohol, pricking it so a bright red drop of blood oozed out.

The blood settled into the groove on the test strip. "29mg/dl."

"Where is Dr. Goshorn?"

"She's right here. Some idiot parked in my place again." The doctor rushed into the room, snapping on latex gloves as the nurse recited the vitals. "I need a bolus of glucagon. And everyone not required to be here, leave." The doctor glanced at Luke before turning to Everleigh. "How's our other patient?"

"She's settled back down. We've got the O2 monitor back on her finger and her vitals are normal."

Luke turned his attention to the second patient in this room. Kariss.

He stood, reluctant to have Everleigh out of his hands. But she needed care his hands couldn't give her now.

He shook his head as logic worked its way through him, dragging with it no small measure of anger.

No one else had access to Charlie's medications.

Who was Everleigh Greene really? And what had he gotten himself into?

LUKE HADN'T WANTED to leave Everleigh alone at the hospital, but they didn't give him a choice. He wasn't family. Her body had been through a significant amount of trauma today, and she would likely sleep through the night. That was his only consolation.

With his heart telling him one thing and his brain arguing the opposite, maybe the best place for him was somewhere else. At least until he could get his emotions in check.

Trying to decide how much he wanted to share with his grandpa, he picked up barbeque sandwiches on the way home.

"You left her all by herself on Christmas Eve?" was the greeting Charlie gave him when he walked in.

"They made me leave. There was nothing else I could do."

"You have a badge."

Luke smiled, but even he knew it was a tired, defeated-looking smile. "Doesn't quite work like that."

Charlie sighed. "I know. Just worried about that sweet girl."

He settled onto the sofa next to Charlie's recliner, leaned back and rubbed his face. "Me too. In fact, I think I could fall in love with her."

"Humph." Charlie snorted. "You don't fall in love. You fall in a ditch. Love is something you choose. If you think that girl is someone you could build a life with, then you fight for it."

"How're you feeling?" Luke changed the subject. He couldn't keep running himself in circles with his current level of knotted up feelings for Everleigh. Charlie didn't know all there was to know about his neighbor, and Luke wasn't ready to tell him. Not on Christmas Eve anyway.

"Like a worn out ol' fool." Charlie returned his recliner to the upright position. "Not much of a Christmas Eve dinner. Not like when Anna cooked for us."

"Weren't a lot of options this time on Christmas Eve." Luke pulled the sandwiches out, then extracted the Styrofoam containers of pickles and sliced onions. Last of all, he set a container of coleslaw in front of his grandpa.

"I didn't mean anything by it. Just missing my Anna more than usual tonight." He lifted the bun from his sandwich and tucked onions and pickles in on top of the chopped brisket. "Whatcha watching?" Luke bit into a sandwich he really wasn't interested in, wondering how much he wanted to tell Charlie about Everleigh. The fact she had stolen Charlie's insulin rattled Luke. His grandpa had suffered. They were lucky some confusion—and an oatmeal-filled coffeepot—was the worst of the damage.

"A televised Christmas Eve service from the old church." Charlie chuckled. "What do ya know. A government official singing a solo at the church. If that don't beat all."

The notes of "Silent Night" filled the room. Luke glanced at the television and paused. It was the same woman he'd seen coming out of the hospital today. "How do you know she works for the government?"

"Tax appraiser. She was at the house just a few days ago."

"This house? Did you let her in?" The hair on the back of Luke's neck tingled.

"Yeah. I made her some sweet tea, and she was nice enough to sit and visit for a bit, even asked to see pictures of Anna. Decently nice lady for a tax officer."

When closed-captioning scrolled her name across the bottom of the screen, Luke jolted upright, his fingers flattening the sandwich he held. Could it be?

Instinct and experience said there was a lot more to Megan's conversation with Everleigh then she'd shared with him. Trudy Wicketts presence at the hospital at the same time as Everleigh's near-fatal overdose didn't feel like a coincidence.

"Did you leave her alone while she was here?"

Charlie thought for a second. "Just for a bit while I went to get some more pictures."

Luke tossed the squashed sandwich on the coffee table. "Where's this church? How far away?"

"Just over on the other side of town. Maybe about twenty minutes. Why? What's the matter?"

Luke calculated in his head. The service was ending. Trudy would have a twenty-minute head start to Brookstone. If she was responsible for what had happened to Everleigh—and his gut told him it was likely—would she return to finish the job?

He wanted to throttle her for taking advantage of his grandpa's loneliness. But if she hurt Everleigh . . .

"Grandpa, I gotta go out for a bit. I want you to keep the doors locked, stay inside, and don't let anyone in."

"What's up, son?"

"No time to fill you in now, but don't worry. There's just one more Christmas present I need to get."

LUKE SLID INTO AN EMPTY spot in the mostly vacant parking garage. The elevator light blinked at the top floor. Not waiting, he took the stairs, his long legs consuming the steps two at a time.

At the second floor, he nearly collided with the detective working Kariss's case.

"What's happened? What's going on?"

"Our girl woke up." The detective's eyes watered. "I believe I've just seen a Christmas miracle."

"What about Everleigh?"

"I didn't know she was still here." The detective scowled. "Something wrong?"

"I hope not." Luke dodged the detective and continued up.

"Does this have anything to do with the case?" The detective followed on his heels.

"I think Trudy Wicketts tried to kill Everleigh."

"That lines up with what we just heard from Kariss. I've put out a BOLO for her vehicle with an alert that suspect is armed and dangerous."

"Can we ping her phone?" A notice to *Be on The Lookout* didn't seem like enough.

"You know something I don't?"

"I have a hunch she might be headed this way."

"Hospital security is on alert."

Though visiting hours were over, no one interfered with his charge to Everleigh's room. He shoved through the door.

"She's awake!" Everleigh's smile practically bounced off every wall to blind him with its brilliance.

The sight arrested him. He wanted to drink it in, but she didn't give him time.

"Her parents were watching the Christmas Eve service on television in her room and when "Silent Night" came on, she woke up."

Chapter Nineteen

Everleigh wanted to fly out from under the covers and race around like Ebenezer Scrooge on Christmas morning.

Only the likelihood of indecent exposure, thanks to the hospital gown she wore, kept her in bed.

She wanted to take hold of Luke and kiss him. Her cheeks warmed at the realization. Remembering where she was and what he was, she tugged the blankets higher, protecting her dignity.

Luke stared, a bewildered expression on his face for a moment. An expression that morphed into the promise of something she sensed but wouldn't dare hope for.

"Detective, can I speak to you outside for a minute?" Luke turned away from her to address Detective Banner. They left the room, taking a part of her joy with them.

Luke returned alone and seated himself on the edge of her bed.

"I need to get out of here," Everleigh said. "It's Christmas Eve, and there's so much I need to do. It won't be much, but will you and Charlie come over for Christmas dinner?"

Luke smiled and shook his head. "Sweetheart, I think you might be getting ahead of yourself. They haven't released you yet."

She narrowed her eyes at him. "Joy killer."

"If I promise to help bust you outta here, will you give me some straight answers?"

"Scout's honor." She held up her hand, palm flat.

"I think that's Heil Hitler," he said, gently lowering her hand and tucking it into his warm grip.

Everleigh swallowed at the understanding her thoughts might not be quite back to normal. "The medication . . . I think maybe . . ."

"Understandable. I deal with this sort of thing all the time." He winked.

"I don't want you to think that I meant to . . ."

"Your secret is safe with me." He squeezed her hand. "Now, how did you end up with an insulin overdose?"

She flinched as he brought her back into the reality that it might be Christmas Eve, but all was not well. Not yet. "Trudy Wicketts. I think she meant to give it to Kariss until I showed up." She licked her lips. "Have you talked to Megan?"

"Yeah, but I don't believe she's telling me everything she knows. Is she involved in this?"

Everleigh nodded. "I don't think she meant to be, but Trudy's blackmailing her. She's scared."

"She's still going to have to answer for what she's done."

"I know. But I think she's truly sorry."

"You could have died."

A faint sheen of moisture glazed his eyes, and it was Everleigh's turn to squeeze his hand. "I didn't. Why?"

"Thanks to Kariss somehow getting her O2 monitor off and triggering the alarm, they found you in time to save you."

"No. I mean, why me when others aren't so lucky?"

Luke released her hand and brushed a strand of hair from her cheek. His voice was husky. "I ask myself that question a thousand times a day. The things I see. They don't make sense when I think of them from the world's perspective. But that's not the perspective we've been called to see the world from."

He sighed, and Everleigh would have climbed into his arms if she'd been dressed in something other than a hospital gown.

"I think we just love the best we can for the time we have. We keep going and giving and believing in a better tomorrow for when our time comes." He looked at her, like he was reaching into his own heart to pull up emotions he'd never shared with anyone before. "Everleigh, do you think we could take a chance on us? I can't promise you the kind of stability you want. My job . . . I can't even promise you a Charlie and Anna kind of love. But I can promise to love you with every day that I am given."

"I think I can learn to live with a little instability if we do it together. Maybe we put this—whatever it is meant to become—and each other into God's hands, every day and for all time."

TRUE TO HIS WORD, LUKE busted Everleigh out—although with a hospital note that it was against medical advice. The bold *AMA* on her chart made her uncomfortable, as though she were breaking the law, until the nurse winked at her and said Merry Christmas.

Holding her hand, Luke escorted her through the parking garage. Everleigh wasn't sure if her feet were actually touching the surface beneath them. She felt too weightless for that.

The artificial light seemed harsh in the dark, cavernous garage, robbing a bit of the Christmas joy with its shadowy corners.

She pressed closer to Luke, holding tightly to his hand.

An engine revved from somewhere in the garage, the sound growling through the cold concrete building. Then the squealing of tires ripped apart the quiet.

Everleigh had heard that sound before, but this time she didn't have a yard to dive into.

They lunged between a couple of parked cars. The short concrete dividing wall was their only option to keep from being crushed. Luke's arm wound around her waist, and he lifted her, launching her over the wall as the sound of ripping metal screamed against the concrete walls.

The cars they'd run between crumpled together, rammed from behind by another vehicle. Luke jumped, rolling himself on top of the concrete wall as the cars slammed against it.

Gunfire cracked. An engine hissed.

"Y'all okay?" Detective Banner shouted. His attention and his firearm aimed at the car.

Everleigh shook when Luke helped her down. He looked at her, and she nodded. He followed Detective Banner, weapon at the ready, as he covered for the other officer.

Sirens rang out in the distance as Trudy climbed from the wrecked car. She followed Banner's commands as though she were in a trance.

"I never meant to hurt her. She made me do it." Trudy's sobbed words wrenched free from a tortured soul. "I only wanted to talk her into getting rid of the baby. It would have destroyed everything my daddy worked to build. It would have ruined Justin's life. Do you see? It had to go away."

Standing by herself, in the dark and grimy parking garage, Everleigh grieved what happened on that horrible night. And then she let go, trusting God would catch each broken piece and one day make everything beautiful again. That was His promise.

And He had wrapped it in a baby in a manger on another night long ago.

That was the reason for the season.

From a car radio nearby the faint notes of a Christmas carol drifted above the melee around her.

Silent night, holy night!
Son of God love's pure light.
Radiant beams from Thy holy face
With dawn of redeeming grace,
Jesus Lord, at Thy birth
Jesus Lord, at Thy birth

She bowed her head and prayed, thanking God for "*the dawn of redeeming grace*" in the birth of her Lord and Savior.

THE END

With her head in the clouds, boots on the ground, and heart in His hands, Lori Altebaumer is a wandering soul with a home keeping heart. She is passionate about God's story of redemption, and it is this passion for the story of good overcoming evil that inspires her love for writing suspense novels. In addition to being an award-winning novelist, Lori also co-hosts the My Mornings with Jesus & Joe podcast with her husband, as well blogging regularly from her website and sites such as Crossmap and The Word on Wednesday. A life-long Texan, she loves being Nana to her grandchildren, things that make her laugh, and real Texas barbeque.

Connect with Lori at www.lorialtebaumer.com[1]

Other Titles:
A Firm Place to Stand
A Far Way to Run
Walking in the Reign: 30 Days of Seeking God's Will

---

1. http://www.lorialtebaumer.com

Don't miss out!

Visit the website below and you can sign up to receive emails whenever Lori Altebaumer publishes a new book. There's no charge and no obligation.

https://books2read.com/r/B-A-FRYI-WNEQC

BOOKS 2 READ

Connecting independent readers to independent writers.

About the Author

Lori Altebaumer shares the joys of Christ-centered living through her writing. An award-winning novelist and Amazon Top New Release author, she writes inspirational fiction, as well as uplifting, faith-based content for Crossmap, The Word on Wednesday, and other online devotions. She also cohosts the *My Mornings with Jesus and Joe* podcast with her husband.

Read more at https://www.lorialtebaumer.com.